'A compulsive piece of reading about a cat who becomes involved in a small farming community's many crises' MANCHESTER EVENING NEWS

'Whether you are a cat lover or not, young Casey, son of a Siamese tomcat and Midge, a black farmcat, is going to claw his way into your heart.
Mrs. Stranger writes with sincerity, a depth of feeling, and poignancy. Undoubtedly this is one of the best animal stories I have read.'
HUDDERSFIELD DAILY EXAMINER

Also by Joyce Stranger

and published by Corgi Books

Joyce Stranger

Casey

CORGI BOOKS
A DIVISION OF TRANSWORLD PUBLISHERS LTD

CASEY
A CORGI BOOK 0 552 08394 1

Originally published in Great Britain by
Harvill Press Limited

PRINTING HISTORY
Harvill Press edition published 1968
Corgi edition published 1970
Corgi edition reissued 1976
Corgi edition reprinted 1977
Corgi edition reprinted 1980
Corgi edition reprinted 1982

This book is set in 11 on 12pt Baskerville

Corgi Books are published by
Transworld Publishers Ltd.,
Century House, 61–63 Uxbridge Road,
Ealing, London W5 5SA
Set, printed and bound in Great Britain by
Cox & Wyman Ltd, Reading

To Kym, our Siamese cat,
who endured many of Casey's mishaps,
and taught me a great deal about cats.

Main Characters

HUMANS

Joe Wayman	owner of Wayman's Corner
Liz Wayman	Joe's wife
Paul Fenton	friend of the Waymans', living nearby in the village
Jill Fenton	Paul's wife
Jane Fenton ⎫ Peter Fenton ⎭	Jill and Paul's children
Lew Martin	seventeen-year-old, employed at Wayman's Corner
Rosie Martin	Lew's mother (no one knows who Lew's father is)
Nat Martin	Lew's grandfather
Ken Lewis	the Vet
Jock Mckie	locum for Ken Lewis
Cliff Howarth	landlord of the Wheatsheaf
Michael Flynn	retired mounted policeman come to live in the village

ANIMALS

Tartar	the Fenton's Siamese tom cat, and Casey's father
Cherry ⎫ Rosie ⎬ Bella ⎭	cows at Wayman's Corner
Starlight	Joe Wayman's bay stallion

Midge	the farm cat at Wayman's Corner, and Casey's mother
Candy	the Fenton children's pony
Tich	Jack Russell terrier at Wayman's Corner
Jokey	Nat Martin's jenny donkey
Sultan	the bull at Wayman's Corner
Nessie } Bennie }	farm dogs at Wayman's Corner
Shanie	Michael Flynn's whippet bitch
Honey	Liz Wayman's mare
Pitch } Toss } Scottie }	ponies at Wayman's Corner
Shadow	Candy's foal

CHAPTER ONE

TARTAR was a Siamese tom cat. Judging by the length of his pedigree and the impressive names that had adorned his ancestors, his blood was as blue as his wicked crossed eyes.

He was slender, and he was elegant, and he knew he was beautiful. He showed himself off to the people who passed by his home, parading for their benefit, never allowing them near. Those he favoured most were treated to a long commentary in his harsh voice, on the weather, on the mice he had caught that morning, and on those he intended to catch before supper.

Sometimes he broke off to abuse a prowling dog. The intruder, ruff bristling, listened in growing astonishment, and then, fury mastering him, gave chase, and Tartar fled, finding sanctuary in the large elm overgrowing the lane. From here, in complete safety, he could continue his insults, until his victim gave up and went off to find easier game.

Tartar's owner, a solicitor in the nearby country town of Glassford, had only moved recently. He wanted a home where his two children could find enjoyment in trees and fields and running streams, and keep a pony in a paddock, and have the responsibility of caring for other live animals. His wife, who had been a model before he married her, was dubious. She loved city ways and city joys. The country was lonely, muddy and wet and full of animals that terrified her.

The cat was wary at first, but soon, finding mice in the orchard and moles in the fields and the paddock, he began to enjoy more freedom than he had ever known. He ranged his new territory, daily amazed by the astonishing beasts that also inhabited this world.

Not only dogs, but cattle and sheep, enormous creatures towering over him, drowning him in their choking scent; hares that fled long-legged up the little slope, too fast for Tartar to catch; rabbits, that, if they were small enough, fell victim to his incessant hunting urge; a fox, leaving his stink behind him to mark that he had passed that way, an overwhelming frightening telltale that the Siamese hated. That day he spent at home, sitting on the window ledge, swearing at invisible creatures, his black tail lashing.

Lew Martin first saw him one green spring day, when the hedges were hazed with promise of leaves to come, and kingcups glittered in the marshy meadow. A thrush in the elm tree flaunted his song, the air dizzy with wild excitement as he rhapsodized the new-warm sun spilling on his feathers.

Lew was seventeen, and, to quote his grandfather, 'only half there nor' by nor' west'. No one in the village was quite sure where the old man found the phrase. He had heard it used in a TV play and it had impressed him. It annoyed his daughter intensely, for Lew, though wanting in the things that most folk held good, such as sums and writing and reading, knew more about wild life and the farm creatures than other men learned in many more years.

Lew himself was unable to explain why he could

not learn his schoolwork, being so tongue-tied with shyness that he could scarcely bear to hear his own voice. He was far from stupid but how could he tell anyone that it was torture to be imprisoned on long dreamy afternoons when the trout were basking in the shallows, and cattle, fetlock deep in mire at the river's edge, swished their tails drowsily, keeping off the summer flies? How explain that when ice held the river in thrall there were birds in need of rescue, some starving for want of food, ducks helpless, their webbed feet frozen to the river's rim, herons needing a hole broken to help them catch the little fish on which they always feasted?

It had been a relief when he was fifteen and could leave school and start on the real business of life, of caring for animals on the farm at Wayman's Corner, where Joe Wayman had inherited a herd of Jersey cattle, and also kept the wicked Jersey bull that was the pride of Lew's life.

He was on his way to the farm at five in the morning, with day dawning, when he saw the cat. Tartar usually distrusted strangers. He acclaimed Lew at once and knew him for a friend, following him, talking in his harsh voice the whole way. Lew had never met a cat with such a voice or such an appearance and he grinned happily and talked nonsense back at the animal.

He was a tall boy, his shock of fair hair bushing over eyes as vivid blue as the cat's, and serene as a pool on a May morning. Nothing worried Lew, but cruelty to animals upset him, and his fury was roused when other people harmed a beast. The village still told the tale of two small boys who had tied a can to a kitten's tail. Lew thrashed them soundly and sent them home, each one with a can tied tightly round his own neck. The village policeman, hearing of the exploit, was afflicted with sudden inexplicable deafness.

Joe Wayman, taking the cows into the yard in front of the milking parlour, stopped to watch, amused, as Lew came up the lane, conspicuous in green trousers and bright red shirt, his old check jacket hanging open. His cloth cap was pushed, as usual, over one ear. He walked loose-limbed through the gate, talking to the cat, who answered every phrase. Lew could always talk to animals, Joe thought, whistling sharply at Cherry, who, caught between Rosie and Bella, was trying to kick her way to greater freedom. It was only humans who made the lad speechless.

'Proper funny lil owd cat, that,' Lew said, dropping his coat on the sack of pony nuts outside the stable. Starlight, a dark bay stallion, handsome as summer, that Joe kept for hunting, heard his voice and thrust his head over the half door, calling a welcome, eager to be fondled. Lew put his head against the horse's neck, pushed his fingers against the warm yielding muzzle, and waited for soft lips to caress him.

That daily and unvarying routine complete, he walked to the milking parlour. Cherry followed him inside, always first, always arrogant, always knowing her place. Tartar, inquisitive, jumped on to a churn, and then jumped down again, and made his way, black tail erect, commenting noisily, towards the stable.

Here he met Midge. Midge was a farm cat, wild, not liking people too near, although, in the cold winter evenings, she expected them to make room for her on the hearthrug and provide her with warm food. In summer she fed herself on mouse and rat families that invaded the haystacks in the barns, and once startled Liz Wayman as she came proudly, dragging a dead but still warm weasel, into the kitchen to show her, as well as showing her mistress the gaping wound that marred her own sleek black fur.

Midge escorted the tom cat to her favourite hunting grounds, and the farm became his second home, so that in no time at all the Fenton children came to look for him there, and Paul Fenton and his wife Jill found an ever-ready welcome in the kitchen at Wayman's Corner. Before the summer ended, Lew helped part-time with the Fenton's pony, fascinated by Candy's gentle ways, and her ready welcome, and pleased to show seven-year-old Jane and nine-year-old Peter, just how to care for their unfamiliar pet.

By the time the first frost blasted the dahlias, Midge was nursing four kittens. Four astonishing kittens, with Siamese bodies and wedge shaped heads, and crossed blue eyes. Except for Casey. Casey was coal black with green eyes like his mother's, but he had Tartar's shape and Tartar's pride, and he soon discovered he had Tartar's voice.

The other three kittens had rusty mews, but Casey had a full-throated yowl that he voiced on his explorations of the farm, when he grew older, but first vented in high-pitched indignation when Midge left him alone in his bed. The other kittens did not constitute company and, moreover, could not satisfy his voracious appetite.

There was no doubt whatever that Casey was the most inquisitive kitten that had ever been born. The world fascinated him from the moment he opened hazed baby eyes, flexed minute but sturdy claws, rolled over his smallest sister, stretched, and fell out of the box in which Midge had so carefully placed him.

From then onwards it was a battle between Casey and Life. As soon as he could stagger he followed Tartar round, admiring the huge Siamese cat that towered above him, and even towered above his mother. Sometimes Tartar would obligingly lift his small son out of danger by the scruff of his neck, but for the most part he left Casey to learn the hard way. And learn the hard way he did.

Wayman's Corner had once been a row of three terraced cottages, and old Tim Wayman, who had died the year before of sheer obstinacy, for no reason at all other than determination to prove the doctor wrong, or so the doctor said, had bought the cottages when they were condemned. Being Tim Wayman he had not knocked them down, but had spent more than he would have done on a new farm, and merged the three into one, making a vast house with a huge warm kitchen which was furnished mainly with saddle racks. Bridles hung over the fireplace, and horse brasses of all kinds decorated every spare patch of wall.

Behind the kitchen, and leading out of it, was a spacious sitting-room, the big comfortable old chairs covered in red rose-blown chintz. Velvet curtains hung floor length over a wall of French windows that looked on to a garden that was a bower of roses, a sea of gold and red and scarlet, of pink and crimson and vermilion, of white and cream and orange and flame.

Here Tim's wife, Pauline, injured in a hunting accident, once watched the seasons come and go as she lay on the big settee. On summer days she could be wheeled out to the rose-clad terrace, where crumbs were put for the birds, and here, when she was alone, she could watch jay and thrush and tit and robin fight with starlings and sparrows and blackbirds for their food. Sometimes a stray squirrel would leap down and grab a crust and dash away again.

She had died six years before her husband, taking away

from him everything that he held good. Liz thought the old man had lost the will to live, and given up trying, and often, as she dusted the sunny room, or drew the thick curtains, she remembered Pauline Wayman, and the brilliant smile with which she greeted her visitors.

She remembered too how her father-in-law had often sat alone in the room, oblivious of those around him, staring out at the garden, and the roses his wife had loved. After his death they took the sitting-room for their main living-room, but it was haunted by sadness, and before long they were back in the busy kitchen, where pups and kittens sprawled on the hearth, and Midge washed her babies, and Tartar often sat on the dresser, ears pricked, eyes alert, watching the turmoil below him.

Casey discovered the sitting-room one bright morning, and discovered the curtains. Liz heard him before she saw him, and looked up to find his black head peering down at her, as he perched on the rail above the window.

'You black demon,' she said, lifting him down. Small threads, torn from the fabric, showed the tracks of his persistent claws.

Midge could show her other kittens where danger lay, but she could not show Casey. He had to find out for himself, had to touch and sniff, and explore, had to discover that the pepper pot on the table made him sneeze, that the spilled beer on the draining board had a foul taste that no amount of milk and water could wash away, that the creosote that Lew used for painting the big fence was disgusting. He sat trying to lick the aftermath away during the whole of one afternoon.

'He must have been born lucky,' Ken Lewis, the Vet, said when he heard about the incident. 'Creosote's poisonous.'

'Born lucky,' became Lew's favourite phrase, as he rescued the kitten time and again from the rafters in the stable. Going up was simple, but how did a cat come down? Casey slipped, and Casey slid, and then he yelled for help. His voice, when he was frightened, was guaranteed to produce results, usually in the shape of Lew, who became his willing slave.

Nothing scared Casey. He met the dogs with friendly advances, and curled up on the hunter's saddle which rested on a rack close to the floor, with Tich, the Jack Russell terrier who was the chief ratter on the farm. The dogs all tolerated the kitten amiably, and helped him spend his immense energy, romping gaily, enduring teasing as he jumped for a pleased and waving tail, and retiring to the sanctuary of the kitchen when he became too rumbustious.

Liz and Joe, veterans of many of Midge's litters, had never known a kitten like him.

'Born to trouble,' Joe said, rescuing him for the second time from the vitals of the washing machine, which lay, dismembered, all over the kitchen floor. He boarded up the hole that led to the works, and that nobody had dreamed was there.

'Born to trouble,' Liz said, brushing dust off her, after crawling under the foundations and rescuing Casey from a cranny that might easily have hidden an outsize rat that would soon have put paid to the kitten's short life. She nailed an extra board vigorously into the space behind the pantry door, while Casey and Tartar watched her with deep interest.

Outside was as dangerous. Joe had covered the well, and made the yard as safe as possible, but no one could cure the kitten of his need to find out for himself. Nobody saw him run, a black smudge on the cobbles, over

to the stable where Starlight was enjoying a late breakfast.

Casey was enthralled. He sat and gazed at this gigantic
and glorious creature, standing splendid, towering to the
roof. One of the hunter's pricked ears was almost as big
as the kitten. One of his long legs offered temptation.
Standing rock-steady, the horse was completely engrossed
in his food.

The kitten began to climb.

Starlight shrilled in protest as small tacks were attached
to him, and unseen claws took a vice-like grip, and pain
needled him. He lashed backwards, and Casey, startled,
gripped tighter.

The horse tried to turn his head and inspect his hindquarters, but the tether held him too tightly. He was always restless indoors, and Joe fastened him to the manger
with a rope with a wooden ball on the end of it. Starlight
was inventive where knots were concerned, and none of
them could restrain him. He often undid them, working
strenuously, and then let himself out of the stable and
spent the night contentedly eating hay.

Casey took a new grip and reached the hunter's rump.

Starlight bucked and Starlight shied and Starlight
kicked, and Joe choked on a mouthful of bacon and bolted to the stables to find his handsome hunter berserk
with rage, unapproachable, squealing his fury, as he tried
to brush a terrified Casey against the wall.

Joe dared not go near. His voice could not reach the
horse, and the kitten was going to be killed.

Starlight bucked again. He twisted, trying to crash the
kitten against the whitewashed bricks, but Casey suddenly
recovered his wits and jumped, and landed, feather light,
in the manger. The horse did not see him. Joe watched
the tiny black scrap claw his way along, and up the

partition. Here he saw refuge and landed without warning on his master's head. He was temporarily a nervous wreck, but all his claws anchored him safely.

Joe bellowed and Liz ran and the stallion squealed again, shouting his fury and indignation at the cavalier way in which he had been treated.

'Born to trouble!' Joe said, when he had time to draw breath. By now Casey was curled on his shoulder, purring endearingly as he savoured warm man, and the safe tweed and tobacco smell, flavoured with horse and cow and bran and chicken mash, that surrounded the farmer in an aura wherever he went.

Liz took the kitten and he purred even more loudly, for Liz was special. She was warmth and love and soft hands and food. Above all, she was food. Warm milk, and steamed fish, and bread soaked in gravy, and slivers of uncooked meat, and the blood from raw liver. Casey, in addition to loving life and loving adventure, also loved to eat, and he ate heartily, so that he was already larger and stronger than his brother and two sisters.

'Your Tartar!' Joe said that evening, when Paul Fenton wandered into the kitchen to find his cat, and share a glass of beer drawn from the barrel that Liz kept providently in the cool cellar beneath the house; 'fathered a demon. Never know what Casey will do next.'

'Nor Tartar either,' Paul said, laughing. 'He spent last night pushing everything on to the kitchen floor. Sugar, tea, three cups, some of Jane's little china animals. Then he apparently chased imaginary mice through the sugar. You should have seen the mess. And him nearly five. You'd think he'd have grown up by now.'

Joe drained his beer mug thoughtfully. He had promised Liz she could keep Casey as well as Midge. If the black scrap turned out anything like his father, as he bid fair to do, it looked as if they were in for a lovely time.

Casey, who had been chasing Tartar's tail, clawed his way up Joe's trouser leg. The Siamese, deceptively meek, greeted his master with raucous joy, and began to lead the way home. Liz never fed him, though she could not always stop him stealing from the dogs. Home, for Tartar, meant food, and after a day on the farm, even on a diet of mouse and rat, the thought of the meal that was always ready for him put eagerness into his step.

Joe, watching them go, the kitten cradled on his arm, looked thoughtfully into the sunset, and scratched Casey's ear.

'Born to trouble, you black demon,' he said.

Casey narrowed his brilliant green eyes and purred even more loudly.

CHAPTER TWO

'You washed?'

Rosie Martin was blonde, like her son, but there all resemblance ended. She was a narrow-shouldered, meanly made woman, her thin hair drawn back tightly from an angular face. The pointed prominent jaw was due, her father said maliciously, to over-much yakking.

Her shrewd blue eyes saw all there was to see, and a good deal more, always putting the worst possible interpretation on every small incident. She was a religious woman, her God a bitter vengeful deity who sided with her in her soreness at an evil world, a world that had mysteriously presented her with a son for whom she could not supply a father.

The cottage where the Martins lived, and had lived for five generations, was immaculate, Rosie being unable to let the dust lie for a second. Her life, as a result, was a running battle. Lew was incorrigibly untidy, and although she nagged him, he could blank her voice out of his mind. Her father, she often said to the sexton's wife, who was her chief crony was enough to plague the wits out of a holy saint in Heaven, let alone hers.

Nat Martin came into the room as she spoke, his boots clumping muddily on the brilliantly polished rose-patterned linoleum. He was a small man, his face plump and creased and shiny, white hair thinly edging his bald head.

'Look at that mud,' Rosie said, her voice shrill with temper.

'Yer'll break me ruddy neck with all yer shimmering and shining,' Nat complained, scraping his chair across the floor, and then pulling it up again to the table, where he sat, expectant and eager.

'You can mind your language in my house.' Rosie was bent over the pans, her face flushed from the heat. She turned to look at him and narrowed her thin lips. Disreputable old thing, she thought irritably. Hadn't polished his boots for nigh on a week, his navy suit was shiny with wear and looking as if he had slept in it and she wouldn't put that past him, not after an evening at the Wheatsheaf. And his old cloth cap was still on his head, and him in her kitchen.

'Take off that cap,' she said.

Nat glowered at her rigid back and flung it across the room to land on a chair.

'And hang it up.'

He clumped over to the peg on the door, deliberately thumping his boots on the floor. It was a losing game. Rosie took the stewpan and ladled the mixture on to three plates, topping each with fat herb dumplings. At least her father kept them well provided with meat, she thought. It had been a good big hare.

Nat's eyes brightened. He loved hare stew, feeling amply rewarded for damp nights spent watching the fields, and noting the runs and laying the snares. It had taken three weeks of cunning to catch this old Wat, but it was worth it. The flavour of stew made his mouth water and he picked up knife and fork as eagerly as a child. Now he was old he loved food more than anything else in the world except Jokey, his old jenny donkey, as grey and worn and weary as himself. And Rosie, for all her nowty ways was a darned good cook. Only virtue she had. He licked his lips and swallowed.

'Nothing's like it used to be,' he said, mouth full of stew. He nodded at Lew, who had just come in, and was washing at the tap in the sink. There was no hot water in the Martins' cottage. Nat repeated the sentence. It was a favourite of his. 'Not had meat for days now. I mind when there was hares by the dozen running in the field at Witchet's Paddock, and Wayman's were alive with rabbits and glad to have ye come and take 'em. And ye could buy six eggs for a penny. And there was six big horses up at Wayman's Corner. Three Shires, two Clydesdales, and a Suffolk Punch.'

'And they hung men at Gallows End,' Rosie said crossly. Heard it all before, near enough night after night for the best part of her life, and fair sick of it.

Nat glared at her. Men came from all over to hear his tales down at the Wheatsheaf. He chuckled. Lies, most of them, and he'd be the first to admit it, but they were based on fact, and dammit, they were good lies. He'd always liked to make a fair job of anything he did.

Even if they'd not hung men in his day they had in his grandad's, and he could remember being nobbut a nipper and standing at the old man's knee and hearing how he'd come home from market and rode up on moor and passed highwaymen swinging in the winter wind. Horses hated Gallows End, even now. Mebbe highwayman did walk as some said. Be sure he'd take the other way home at night. Funny how much more sensitive a man was after a pint or two. Good for the eyes and ears, beer was, making you hear sounds you'd never hear else, and see things too. And specially good was the beer at the Wheatsheaf, and nigh on opening time. He jingled his money, and left the table.

Lew had finished his meal too. He was going back to the farm with a gift for owd bull, and then mebbe he'd show Peter and Janey how to jump with Candy, though, come to think, Candy was getting a mite fat, and mebbe she'd have a foal and they oughtn't to ride her. He ought to tell their Mam only it was a tricky thing to tell a lady and he didn't much like to. Mebbe Candy was just getting too much food and too little exercise. Jumping would do her a world of good, and the kids'd enjoy it. Proper clever little riders they were getting. He reached for his cap.

'Now where you going? Never at home. Treat me like a landlady,' Rosie said, snappish, lacking company.

Lew ignored her, and slammed out of the door. It was easier not to answer. There was nothing to keep him at home, the chairs as hard and comfortless as the floors, and his mother for ever smoothing the cushions that sat fat and unyielding behind his back. His own room was a tiny slip of a place with a hard mattress and iron bedstead and a chair and the little cupboard in the wall for his few clothes.

Nat had hired a television set, paying for it out of his pension, but often Rosie sat watching it alone, her father at the Wheatsheaf and Lew out. What boy wanted to be stifling indoors when there were trout to guddle down at the weir and hares to watch, and owd bull to talk to? Wasn't worth staying with his mother anyway. Grouse. Grouse. Grouse. If she'd been Liz Wayman now—

Lew loved Mis' Liz almost as devotedly as he loved owd bull, but he would rather die than admit it. She did not even suspect the admiration behind the gifts he brought her – a bunch of bluebells, snowdrops tangled with mud, kingcups from the river meadow, a lapwing's egg, found in the far field, perhaps dropped by a marauding magpie. To her, Lew was only a boy, too young to know the miseries of adult life.

Lew loved owd bull. He was a splendid creature of towering strength, capable of ferocity, yet as gentle with Lew himself as a ewe with her newborn lamb. He was magnificent, a glorious beast, the most wonderful occupant of Lew's world, his sultry temper brooding over the farmyard, everyone all the time conscious of him there, of his long periods of glooming, and of his sudden rages. He was a symbol of everything that Lew himself lacked, of power, of personality, of domination. His name was Sultan, his pedigree impressive. Jersey bulls have infamous reputations and owd bull had no intention of letting down the breed. The boy could never see enough of him, and often, when Joe missed him, and there were chores yet to be done, he would find the pair of them holding silent conversation.

When owd bull was grouchy, Lew alone could quieten him. He stared at the small bright eyes, sparking with anger, the lowered head, the sweeping horns. At the huge humped shoulders, swaying as the raging head swayed, at the horn tip angling at the door. Sometimes Sultan heralded his fury with the crash and rend of splintering wood.

'Poor owd bull,' Lew would say and his hands would move, fondling the thick wrinkled neck, gentling, soothing, stroking with soft sweeping movements. The swaying head stilled. Owd bull snorted and Lew dipped his face and rubbed his cheek against the massive head. Owd bull grunted.

It never failed, and Joe never failed to mutter as he watched.

'It's a ruddy miracle.'

Away from the farm Lew's world was also Nat's world, sky and moor, and woodland where squirrels chattered and the owl swept low at night calling his ghost cry as he flew. Owd hare fled up the furrow and owd fox fought and foraged and taught himself how to fool the Hunt and how to live until another day.

Down by the rushing rivers that rippled and splashed, criss-crossing the mud-banked edges of the flood plains, owd otter darted through the water, or sank to leave his glittering bubble trail, or flashed with his otterlets down the little weir, offering a brief glimpse of sleek dark heads and shining eyes and slender bodies that were miracles of grace.

Tonight Lew had a gift for owd bull. He felt infinite pity for the beast, cooped for ever in his pen, on hard ground, with no soft field to roam in. With such a savage temper, Joe Wayman did not dare let him run with the cows. Too many people used the right of way across the cattle field. A confounded nuisance it was, especially in summer when townsfolk would drive their cars across his grazing and park beside the river to picnic, and leave their muck and broken bottles for his beasts to cut themselves on.

Lew took his gift into the yard. A pail full of fresh cut green grass. Owd bull was day-dreaming, peaceable for once, his small eyes watching nothing, his immense bulk melting into the dusk behind him, his breath warm on Lew's face. He turned his head at the sound of the boy's voice, and then brightened. Between him and the farm hand there was always this immediate bond that nobody else could fathom.

Lew held out the grass and the bull began to eat, revelling in the rough hand that caressed his head, and soft words that soothed him. The steel and concrete pen bore signs of his fury. A dented rail, from an angry horn. Marks on the wall from kicking hooves. The week before he had pulled his nose rope out of Joe's hands with such savagery that the rough fibre had gashed the skin, leaving a raw patch that looked as if it had been flayed.

Liz hated him. One day he would kill one of them, she knew, and she rarely passed the bull pen without a shudder.

'Please sell him,' she begged, over and over again, but Joe only laughed. He was a good bull, a splendid bull, and his daughters were wonderful milkers and fetched high prices. You only had to watch out. . . .

But Liz still remembered one bright day two years before. The bull had been in the yard with Cherry all day, and when the cow went back to pasture Joe took Sultan's nose rope to lead him into his pen. She had been collecting eggs.

As she crossed the yard Sultan twisted his head and angled his horn towards her. Terrified, she backed away, and fell across the mounting block. That night her baby was born, more than two months too soon. She could not bear to think of it, even now, or of the small grave on the tree-shaded hillside under the shelter of the grey stone church that she attended each Sunday. Or of the specialist's words. No more children possible. Ever.

Surrounded by fertility, she was as barren as Nat Martin's old grey jenny, Jokey. The men joked about that, but it was a poor joke at best. She dug her trowel viciously into the ground between the pansies, stooping over the flower bed. Today her son would have been two years old.

Lew hoped that she would speak to him, but she kept her back turned. He fed owd bull and rested his head against the animal's neck, remembering how wicked he was. How he had kicked the sheltie across the yard when it barked at him, and how he had tried to trample Midge under stamping furious hooves. The little cat had only just escaped in time, and never been near the bull pen since. Even Tartar gave him a wide and wary berth, after one brief encounter. He had been exploring the rafters and jumped down in the bull pen. Sultan bellowed and thrust out his horn. Tartar, terrified, leaped backwards over the half-door and sat outside, recovering, his tail fluffed to five times normal size, his body shaking, his voice lifted in bitter upbraiding that served to anger the bull still more, so that he squealed in rage and pawed the ground and tried to fling himself at the cat.

Owd bull was sleepy. Lew had fed him and soothed him, and for a little while he forgot the confines of his stall, and the strange existence that he led. He dreamed of his youth, of his calf days in the yellow-green meadows, of the bliss of standing deep in the racing river, the water cool to hot hooves, and bending to drink, savouring the taste, which was not like the bucket-tainted taste of the water he drank now.

Casey, bored with the yard, and seeing Lew, sidled up to him. Lew bent to stroke him, but the kitten wanted more than that, and leapt to the boy's shoulder. Here, startled, he gazed straight at the bull and the bull stared back. Lew was paralysed, waiting for disaster. He moved away, but Casey leaped to the half-door and patted the bulls's face with an inquisitive paw.

Sultan snorted, and glared at the kitten. Liz, turning, saw the pair of them and caught her breath. One more second, and the bull would sweep Casey out of this world with his horn. She dared not speak. Lew stood stock-still, his eyes anguished, afraid to move. Casey began to purr.

27

The full-throated Siamese sound filled the air with content. The bull half closed his eyes. The companionable noise pleased him. Casey sensed warmth. The bull's hide was soft. His neck looked comfortable. The kitten jumped, and, landing, curled himself up small, his purr throbbing even more loudly.

'Oh Casey!' Liz said.

Sultan turned and eyed the cat. He could just reach the little animal. He stared at the kitten for a moment, and then his long tongue came out and licked Casey's head.

'Owd bull . . . he likes that lil owd cat!' Lew exclaimed, surprise for once allowing him to voice his thoughts to Liz.

That night Casey slept on the bull's back, and from then onwards, if he was ever missing, he was sure to be found in the bull's pen, the pair of them utterly content. Casey's blissful purr filled the air, and owd bull every now and then would turn and lick the little beast, finding in him the companion that he had always lacked.

'Dang me,' Nat said, a few weeks later, down at the Wheatsheaf, 'that lil owd cat and owd bull's like drinking mates . . . that fond of one another.' But the men at the Wheatsheaf were used to Nat, and smiled tolerantly, classing this fable as yet another of his famous lies.

'Has a wayward tongue, owd Nat,' they said, after he had gone home, taking care to avoid Gallows End.

'Tells the truth sometimes.' Cliff Howarth, the landlord, was not long come to Petley Green, only been there for five years, fresh from a backstreet London pub. He was a dark burly man, overfilling his clothes. He looked contentedly at the country faces, at the rough wood benches and scarred tables of the public bar, and through the hatch at the black oak of the inner room where he served food that people came from miles away to sample. His pies were so good that he found himself with regular orders from the village wives on Mondays.

'Known a horse take up wi' a cat, but not a bull,' one of the men said. 'And that bull of Joe Wayman's ... stone me! He's a devil.'

'Time now,' Cliff Howarth said.

The last goodnights echoed in the lane outside, and Cliff went to look at the new moon and turn his money in his pocket. Funny little cat that, up at Wayman's. Visited the Wheatsheaf once or twice with Joe, and liked to lick the froth off the beer.

Cliff barred the door and began to clear up.

He turned, startled, as the knocker thundered.

Outside the door Joe Wayman faced him, his face white, a long gash across his forehead dripping blood on to his jacket collar.

'Ring the folk around for help,' he said, his voice conveying urgency in a way that words could not. 'Some little loon from the town came by the farm tonight, drunk as a lord, and he's let the bull out. Came to see the kitten and the bull.'

'He'll be the little tick I threw out an hour ago,' Cliff said, furious at himself for not having seen how the wind blew earlier. The youngster had been there with a girl, showing off, and she egging him on. He'd got right sick of the pair of them.

'Where's the bull now?'

'God only knows. And watch out for the ambulance. Direct them to the farm, will you, Cliff? Liz hasn't time to phone for help – she's got her hands full.'

'Ambulance?' Cliff stared, stupid. It had been a long day and he was tired.

'Idiot boy took a stick to the bull. What the hell d'you

think happened? Bull broke the half door, didn't even think it possible, and went for him. I got him off with the pitchfork, but not before he'd had a go at me with his horn, and he broke down the gate and got away. And that black kitten of mine as well, off like a bat out of hell, too.'

Joe stormed away, raging. Gears screamed, anguished, as he drove away at full throttle, anxious to catch the runaway.

Cliff picked up the telephone, mentally ticking off names of the nearby farmers. Back at the farm Casey crept home alone and slipped into the empty bull-pen and cuddled into the straw, unable to understand the commotion of people and vehicles round the farm in the middle of the night.

CHAPTER THREE

THE bull had been watching the last swallows when the little red sports car skidded to a standstill. He heard the mocking voices, but they meant nothing. The two came through the gate, the boy highly elated, the beer and whisky inside him at war with his senses, the girl half afraid, wanting to egg him on, yet scared. This was danger, this was more frightening than racing at sixty miles an hour down the lanes with the roar of the wind in her face and her hair flying and her teasing voice urging for speed and yet more speed, faster and faster, until they were spinning through the night and the boring old world was temporarily forgotten, a flashing blur, only half glimpsed as they fled.

'I'm a bullfighter. Going to fight the old bull.' The boy was a dandy, his clothes glove-tight, his hair long and silken, finespun on his shoulders, a small black moustache giving his face an improbable elegance that would have been dashing were the hair cut short. He minced on black patent leather points, found a bamboo among those that Liz had been using to stake the plants and flashed it, swordlike, his wrist flexing as he turned and bent and bowed.

'There *is* a cat on the bull. For God's sake,' he said, and jabbed. The girl laughed. Casey, caught in his tender midriff by the stick, gave an outraged yowl, clawed at the bull, and then leaped to safety, high in the rafters. Ears flattened, he swore, long and loud and viciously. The bull, incensed by the noise and the tearing claws, pawed in anger, and humped his shoulders and lowered his head.

'Who's afraid of the big bad bull? The big bad bull? The big bad bull? Who's afraid of the big bad bull? Not I. Not I. Not I.'

He was dancing, spinning, twisting, turning, looking to the girl for approval, his teeth flashing white in his flushed brown face, his eyes glittering at her, derisive.

'I'm a bullfighter, a hero, and I lay my prowess at your feet.'

He bowed again, and took off his jacket, stepping backwards, turning, circling, spreading the cloth as he had seen the bullfighters spread their capes.

'I'm going to let him out. Poor old thing, cooped up there. He's got a rope on his nose. Let's take him to those cows in the far field. Poor old bull, stuck away from cows. Wouldn't do for me, would it, love?'

He was mocking her, and she hated him and loved him, and she was afraid for him, and yet she wanted him to fight the bull. She stood at the edge of the yard, her dress a white blur against the dark railings.

He turned and poked at the bull with the stick. Sultan had never been so outraged in his life. He humped himself and pushed against the door.

'Poor old fellow. Don't know what life is,' the boy said. He laughed, flicked the bull on the shoulder, and put his hand to the latch on the door, slipping it out of its groove. He smiled at the girl, who had retreated to the farthest corner of the yard.

'Scaredy cat.'

He was brave, he was valiant, he was a hero, he was on top of the world, outdoing all its great men. He could drive faster, run fleeter, fight harder than any of them and he could conquer the bull.

He pirouetted, turning on his heel, spreading his coat.

'Olé!' he shouted.

The latch slipped as Sultan thundered into the yard, smashing the half door against the side of the pen. One hinge gave. The door sagged to the ground.

The whisky bravery was fading. The bull was immense, a mass of power and anger. The boy hesitated, dropped his coat, and was lost as the great beast charged him, lifted him on one pointed horn and then trampled on his victim, all the pent anger of the last few minutes finding outlet. Casey was swearing inside the pen. The girl's screams deafened the night. The two shelties added their uproar to the din.

Joe, who was exercising the hunter in the far field, heard the outcries. He galloped full pelt. As Starlight jumped the fence into the yard the bull panicked. He did not like the sudden apparition of horse and man coming towards him, and Liz had set the dogs on him. Tich barked at one side, and Nessie at the other. The chained dogs kept up a constant deafening clamour. He turned towards the gate, which shuddered at his impact, and then he was gone, with a rending of wood and a thump of hooves on the hard road outside. The yard was a shambles.

It was dark, and rain was beginning. The bull had not been subjected to weather for seven long years. He did not like rain, did not like the unfamiliar hedges about him, nor the weasel that scurried, almost under his feet, and vanished into the bank at the laneside. He hated the sudden noise of an inquisitive horse, galloping to look at him, curious, and then keeping him company, cantering alongside, huffing over the hedge.

There were strange scents on the air. There were fox smells and flower smells, the stench of a rat dead in a ditch, the rotting smell from a stagnant pond. And then the exciting telltale of warm cattle. He flung back his head. Cows were near him. Not his own familiar herd, but another. He tried to plough through the ditch but the fence was strong and resisted him. An enchanting red and white pedigree Ayrshire put her warm nose over a gap and licked him. He stayed with her for a little, and then a lorry came up the hill, gears screeching as the driver changed down, clumsy with tiredness after too long a day on the road, flouting the regulations to earn more overtime and take home good money to his wife and six children.

The gears startled the bull, and he cantered on, turning into the narrow lane that led to Holden's workings. A moment later, he was at the entrance to the sand pits. He stopped, puzzled. The watchman saw him, and shouted and fled for the telephone.

The bull did not like people. He did not like unfamiliar voices or loud noises, and tonight he had heard them all. He fled again, his heart thumping with terror, as his hooves trampled the narrow hard packed sandy way, past a huge crane that raised its jib high above him, threatening, he thought, to come down and crush him. Panic-stupid, he thudded on, until the slow slope ended and he fell, up to his neck in icy water.

The shock took his breath away. He stood there for almost five minutes before he recovered his wits and tried to struggle out of the pool. He shook his head vigorously, and then began to call, his high pitched squeals begging for help.

34

The watchman, hearing him, came cautiously, and then stared.

'Well, feller, you're in a proper pickle,' he said, scratching his head in bewilderment. 'How in hell do we get you out o' there?'

He was an old man, a small man, his grey hair sparse, his beaky nose mottled, his thin lips drawn back in a caricature of a grin that misled people into assuming affability that was not there until they realized it was a habit, a nervous trick, a fear grin with which he hoped to placate a world that was bewilderingly hostile. He had worked for the council, on the roads, until retirement, and now he spent his nights guarding the equipment at the sand workings. Though what good he might be except for his telephone, he did not know, and no one else had considered.

He went back to the telephone.

'Got bored, have you?' the duty sergeant asked sourly, as he heard old Stan's voice again. Silly old fossil. Saw hobgoblins in the shadows half the time and thought they were thieves come to steal the equipment. It did not occur to the sergeant that the old man felt vulnerable and was frightened, out there, miles from anywhere, and no one to help him if trouble did break. If there'd been money now, you'd not catch old Stan Mossop there alone at night, not for a king's ransom.

'Bull's in the water up to his neck,' Stan said.

'O.K. We'll be there.' The sergeant rang off and cursed. Joe Wayman had already reported the incident. All this trouble because of a drunken little tick who should have been leathered twice a week by his father and then maybe he'd have grown up with some sense in him. The sergeant believed in 'spare the rod and spoil the child' and said so, often, earning himself a number of nicknames that it was as well he did not hear.

He had a cup of tea beside him, now almost cold, and he swallowed it, pulling a grimace of distaste as he gave his orders over the telephone. The fire brigade were used to animals in trouble. The men knew what to do. He sighed with relief and stretched himself.

Had to fill in his report. Called to Wayman's Corner. And there was one little fool who would be no trouble for a bit. Crushed ribs and damaged leg. Concussion, and God knew what had happened to his insides when a ton of mad bull jumped on him. And the girl. Hysterical women were the limit and half the women he met seemed to have cause to make them scream and cry. He had slapped her face in desperation. Might have been a pretty little thing if you washed that muck off her, and it had run down her cheeks. A right sight she looked. Dammit to hell, and the night only just begun, the sergeant thought sourly.

He dragged open the drawer. Cheese and onion. Limited mind, his wife had. What he'd like would be a nice piece of beef in his sandwiches, cut thick, half raw and juicy, spread with horse radish cream. And a meringue. He just fancied a meringue. He had a sweet tooth. He sighed. To hell with it.

Called to Wayman's Corner at 9.15.

The room was silent except for the ticking clock and his scratching pen.

Nat Martin was sitting in a field, sheltered under the hedge, when he heard the bull crash past. He had not gone straight home when he left the Wheatsheaf, but taken the winding lane to avoid Gallows End. Also there was a hare in the Long Meadow. He wanted a closer look.

And then the bull came. Owd bull from up at Wayman's, owd devil bull – and him loose. Nat turned for home, hastening to find Lew, who could handle the brute. His old legs would not run fast enough and he slipped and fell in the mire and swore and picked himself up, and hurried on, his breath torturing his lungs.

Lew was asleep. Lying on his back, legs wide, arms wide, bare to the waist, he lay staring blindly at the ceiling. Nat shook him, his lungs harsh with noise. Lew woke.

'Owd bull's got out,' Nat whispered, the words coming with difficulty. He felt that he could never breathe in comfort again. Sweat poured off his face.

'Owd bull!'

Lew grabbed his clothes and pulled them on. Owd bull was his concern, his wonderful powerful beast. He might get hurt. He might run into a lorry, or fall in a ditch. He might be shot.

Rosie heard them go and shouted, but no one heeded her. She glared at the slammed front door, and huddled back into bed, her mouth grim. She'd have words with them in the morning, the pair of good-for-nothings. Though perhaps if they brought her a hare. . . . Only the thought of meat that would keep her money in her purse ever sweetened Rosie. She went back to sleep.

Nat led the way at first, but soon dropped back, wondering if the stitch in his side would kill him.

'Towards the sand pit,' he said.

Lew began to run. The sand pits were dangerous. Lads had drowned in the waterfilled quarries which were no longer worked. A horse had drowned there too. He remembered seeing it floating on the surface, rigid and bloated. Fear sent him sprinting across a ploughed field, hurdling the fence, racing across the road, and into the quarry. Behind him the fire engine's siren shrieked like a demented banshee as it sped along the narrow winding lanes.

The bull heard the noise too, and lowed in anguish. He was icy cold, and the water terrified him. If he moved, his hooves sank into sand, and water flooded his nostrils. He arched his neck backwards, lifting his head as high as was possible, and bellowed again, calling for assistance.

Lew heard him and shouted. The bull knew Lew's voice, knew the familiar ring of his own name, and answered, sure that now all would be well, and he would soon savour the dark and welcome warmth of his familiar pen, the rustle of clean straw under his hooves, the gentle warmth of the little cat curled on his back.

'Poor owd bull,' Lew said, appearing out of the night.

He wanted to cry, for there was his magnificent beast muddied and his pride humbled, his strength useless. He was helpless as a new calf, standing there in the water. His eyes begged for rescue.

Lew waded into the pool.

'Eh, lad, you're daft,' the old watchman said. He had been back to his hut to telephone Wayman's Corner. He knew Joe, and he had recognized the bull for a Jersey beast. No one else kept Jersey cattle. Sultan's temper was a byword in Petley Green. Everyone knew what had happened to cause Liz to lose her baby.

Lew was tall, but even so the water came chest deep. He turned his shoulder, and Sultan rested his head. It was pleasant to relax muscles which ached from holding it above the water. Nat, stumbling, almost exhausted, towards the shine of the watchman's torch, gasped as he saw his grandson.

'Eh, our Lew, you're daft,' he said, in the watchman's words, and Lew, after a moment's thought, grinned at him. The fire engine would soon be here, and there would be rescue for both of them. He began to croon to the bull. He could feel the beast trembling, or was he shivering?

If he died of cold . . . or caught a fever . . . Lew began to shiver himself at the thought. He stroked the soft neck, and rubbed his face against the bull's head.

Joe Wayman, racketing to a standstill with a screech of protesting brakes as he skidded the Land-Rover, saw Lew and gasped.

'Eh, lad, you're daft,' he said, and Lew laughed outright. Three of them, he thought. All with the same words. That was right funny.

Joe looked at his bull. The fire engine was closer. He could hear the thud of noise from the engine and the scream from the siren. If the bull caught cold . . .

'Seven hundred guineas I paid for that bull. He's a damn good bull,' he said fiercely to the nightwatchman.

The old man chewed on his false teeth and did not answer. Seven hundred guineas for a dumb animal, dear God, and him without seven hundred halfpennies to bury him decent when his time came. Some people didn't know they were born.

'Going back to me hut. Nowt I can do here,' he said querulously. 'Make yer some tea. Time to brew up,' he added as an afterthought.

'Do better with brandy,' Joe said. There was a bottle in the Land-Rover. Useful for all kinds of emergencies including those involving animals. He handed it to Lew.

'Take a swig of that to keep the cold out,' he said.

Lew accepted the bottle doubtfully. He stared at it before uncorking it, and then, after a moment's thought, poured the better part of the contents into the bull. The animal choked and shuddered, but the fiery stuff went down his upturned throat.

'Waste of good brandy.' Nat's eyes were greedy.

Lew tasted it, and spat.

'Put some down you, lad,' Joe said, urgent. Be a fine

caper if the boy got pneumonia as a result of the night's work. One serious casualty was bad enough. The lad who'd let the bull out had been a right old mess. Joe shuddered. He still felt sick, even though they said the boy would live. And no one was going to make him get rid of his bull, he thought, obstinate as his father, Tim Wayman's son, every inch of him. Rather die than confess he was wrong. The bull was a good beast, and it was not his fault he'd got loose.

The fire engine braked. Men spilled out of it, fixing floodlights, which made the bull low in terror. Everything was strange tonight. Lew stroked him, murmuring reassurance. Poor owd lad. Poor owd feller. No one'll hurt yer. It was easy to talk to owd bull, like talking to a little lad, just murmur and comfort him, and he was as quiet as a new kitten. Liked hymns too, owd bull did. Lew began to sing under his breath. He did not know the words, but he liked the tunes, and one of the men fixing the lamps stared at him in astonishment as he began to hum 'Lead kindly light'.

The scarlet Land-Rover that braked behind the fire engine backfired as the engine stopped, making everybody jump. Ken Lewis climbed out, long legged, thickset in his sheepskin jacket, his dark hair unbrushed and straight on end above a large knob-ended nose. His brown eyes, half hidden behind thick glasses, were angry.

'Fine thing to happen,' he said. 'Want to lose that bull?'

'Some stupid little drunk let the damned beast out,' Joe said angrily. 'Nothing to do with me.'

'Your bull.' Ken Lewis hated night calls, and there were a sight too many of them. He needed a partner. Needed a night's sleep too, and now this night as good as gone. Take the best part of it to get a brute that weight back on dry land, and then in the horse box, and then he'd need drying and an anti-shock injection and constant care for a few days.

The watchman came back with a mug of tea.

'Only got one mug. Drink oop, lad,' he said, and passed the mug to Lew who drank it gratefully. Better than the brandy. His body was becoming numb, his legs turned to icy blocks that refused to obey him, and the bull's head had trebled in weight in the last few seconds.

'Not be long now, lad,' one of the firemen said. 'Think you can fasten the slings?'

Lew nodded, but when he tried to handle them his hands were too cold and he dropped them. One of the firemen walked into the water, eyeing the bull doubtfully.

'Can't do you no harm there, Nick,' a jocular voice said from the bank.

'This cold will. Chill the life from you,' the man grumbled. 'Eh, lad, rather you than me.'

Lew's teeth were beginning to chatter. He could feel the bull shivering too, tremendous rib-shaking shudders that shook both of them. He tried to tighten his grip and sing again, but he was too numb and too cold. He and owd bull would die there, die of chill, and never run around again, not either of them. And what would Casey do, Lew wondered. That lil owd cat, he fair doted on owd bull.

'All right, lad,' one of the men said. 'We're pulling. Out you come,' and he reached out his hand. Lew took it and found his legs would not move so that two of the men waded in beside him and half carried him out of the water.

'Towel in my car,' the Vet said. He hurried off and reappeared with a change of clothing that he kept for unusually dirty jobs. Not very clean but at least they were dry. He gave Nat the towel, and watched until the old man had stripped off the boy's wet clothes and begun to rub him down.

'Try using that.' He handed his woollen scarf to Lew. It wouldn't dry much but it would make the boy move his limbs and help restore the circulation. A fireman was helping Nat rub the lad, and the watchman, who had vanished, now re-appeared with a thick hooded navy-blue duffel coat.

The bull, deserted, lifted his head and cried his desolation to the stars.

CHAPTER FOUR

LIZ, left alone at Wayman's Corner, made herself a cup of coffee, and sat by the dying ashes to drink it. She was tired, and she felt sick. The boy's moans and the girl's screams still rang in her ears. All the lights were on in the yard, the bull's pen illuminated by a lamp hanging from the corner. Rays from the milking parlour flooded across the blood-stained cobbles.

She ought to switch them off. She ought to go to bed. Joe would never wake to start milking in time. Instead, she dreamed on, and Midge sidled in through the door and settled herself in the hearth, her tail almost in the ashes, her small purr contented as she curled to sleep. Liz yawned. The clock struck the half hour. Half past twelve. She moved towards the staircase, only part of her mind on bed.

The bull would need deep straw in his pen when they'd hauled him out of the water. He'd be soaked, and chilled, and in danger of pneumonia. If he died . . . if he died they could claim the insurance, and live without a bull. The heavy animal was too big for the heifers. The A.I. man had to see to those. He could do the whole herd, even if Joe did insist the rate of failure was too high with artificial insemination, and the cost prohibitive when you had your own bull anyway.

The insurance. Liz ran to the desk, and turned over the papers. Joe had asked her to renew the insurance. When? She found the right paper and stared at the date. The thing was overdue by nearly three weeks. How could she have forgotten? And when Joe found out. . . .

Sleep was out of the question. Liz walked outside. The wind was rising, keening in the trees that acted as a break on the nearby field. It whipped at her skirt and her hair, and teased the ends of straw in the haystack. The world was alive with wild cloud chasing across the moon, and with the sough and rush and whistle of fast moving air. Starlight pawed restlessly in his loose-box. He hated wind.

And he was still saddled and needed grooming and feeding. How could she have forgotten? Cursing, Liz ran upstairs, changing quickly into jeans and an old jersey. She hated grooming the stallion. He was impatient with her, preferring Joe or Lew. He pawed the straw restively, twisted away from her, and sometimes tried to bite. But it had to be done.

She was relieved to see that he was extremely tired and also hungry. She measured his feed and put it in the manger, and let him eat while she removed the saddle, and then began to brush the worst of the evening's dust and mud from him. He was too hungry to care. Once, as she tried to ease a tangle from his tail, he turned and looked at her, but he quieted again, and she was able to give him extra straw for bedding and shut him up without any trouble.

Just as well, she thought. She could not have endured a struggle at that time of night.

The bull-pen was next. No one had mucked it out yet, and she fetched fork and broom and barrow and began the uncongenial task. Casey followed her, wailing, his Siamese voice in full cry. Twice she wondered if some-

44

thing more was wrong than the missing bull, and then as Casey yowled again and stared at her reproachfully, she heard the dogs whining.

Joe had shut them in the barn, out of the way of ambulance and police car. She went to release them, and Casey ceased his noise and greeted Tich as if the Jack Russell had been separated from him for weeks. Liz forked the last of the soiled straw into the wheelbarrow and pushed it over to the midden. Nessie followed her, joyous at release, and Bennie, the farm guard dog, solemn and responsible, sat and watched them, his tail wagging his approval. He was a handsome dog, a Labrador-retriever cross, with more intelligence than any mongrel Liz had ever known.

When Joe was away for the night Bennie was Liz's protector, and knew that this night he did not sleep outside, but lay on guard at the stair head, growling gruffly at any unfamiliar noise. When Joe was home he slept in the hay, lying on straw against the piled bales, ready to bark a warning should any intruder come by.

He watched benevolently as Nessie followed Liz to and fro, as she brought bales from the stack and split the twine and spread the straw to make a thick warm bed on which the bull could lie. Whatever happened, he mustn't die now. Seven hundred guineas, and she had forgotten the insurance. She stabbed at the straw angrily.

She did not notice Tich. He always accompanied Joe, sitting in the Land-Rover on the passenger seat, his ears cocked, his bright eyes watching the road. He had never been left at home in the whole of his two years. He nosed around the yard, following the trail of the Land-Rover wheels, and decided to find his master. He slipped through the gate. Casey, curious, followed him, closer than a shadow.

They hurried through the darkness, Casey running to keep up, his tail erect, his ears alert for any strange sound or movement. Tich trotted solemnly, his blocky body determined, moonlight shining on the white patches that broke the ginger brown of his short thick fur. His stump tail wagged as he nosed the surface of the lane.

The sand pits lay bleak under the moon. Light glinted on water, reflected machinery, blinking as clouds scudded over the sky. The needling wind was cold. Lew went to sit in the watchman's hut, where a slow combustion stove gave welcome heat. Joe walked into the water, shivering. It would help if three of them pushed the beast. The bull lowed miserably, by now so exhausted that the sound was a bleat of despair. Lew had looked at him sadly, for he was no longer arrogant in his nobility, but a lonely, frightened and miserable animal, content to rely on the men around him to rescue him from his predicament.

Tich saw his master standing in the water and barked his outrage. Joe saw the small dog running frantic, along the edge of the pit.

'Shut up, blast yer,' someone growled, irritation exploding. Tich went on barking.

The bull lowed again. Casey heard the sound and stared around him. He loved the bull more than anything in the world, finding company in the beast, and warmth, and affection. He yowled, loud and long.

'Strewth,' one of the firemen said. 'Sounds like a devil.'

'Blasted cat,' the watchman said morosely. He hated the critturs, hated their soft footed approach, loathed the creepy way they slipped up on you, loathed the feel of their fur, detested their strange accusing eyes. Casey, as if he knew this, weaved a pattern round the man's legs, and he shoved the cat away with his boot, pushing hard. Casey

46

swore at him, fur fluffed, ears flat, eyes outraged.

'Damned brute,' the watchman said, and walked away. The bull lowed.

Casey turned towards the sand pit, and saw him standing up to the neck in the water. The cat hated water. He began to pace along the edge, howling, his voice louder and louder as he realized the enormity of what had happened, and saw the gap between him and Sultan.

There was no sign of temperament now. When the sling tightened and the crane began to lift, the bull did not resist. He felt the water slide away from him and lowed softly, frightened in a new way by the strange sensation of swinging into the air and on to the bank again. Joe climbed wearily after him. Casey rushed to them, and rubbed against Sultan, his small tongue licking urgently at soaking fur. The bull lowered his head and greeted the cat with a long pink tongue.

'Stone me!' one of the men said.

Joe took the towel and rubbed some of the water from himself, standing patiently, dripping from every garment, as Ken Lewis gave the bull first a tranquillizing injection and then another against shock.

'Get him into the trailer,' he ordered, and the beast cried out in fear as the sling tightened again and he was lifted, to stand unsteadily beside the horse box. Hard hands pushed him. Meekly he stumbled inside. Casey followed, flashing past them, settling himself beside the bull. Ken Lewis climbed in, and called to Lew, who had come out of the hut.

Joe humped into the driving seat, water streaming from his clothes. A moment later they were off, going as fast as was feasible over the bumpy track, turning into the lane, jolting along the road, and into the farmyard gate. Liz was waiting for them, the bull-pen was ready for them, and a steaming jug of cocoa, plentifully laced with rum, was standing on the Aga, keeping hot.

Joe changed out of his wet clothes, rubbed himself dry, swallowed his drink, and went out to the yard, to help with his bull. He and Lew and Ken worked side by side, using straw rolled into balls in their hands, rubbing water from the beast's hide, working to restore the circulation to numbed limbs and shivering body. Casey sat on the bull's shoulder and added his small contribution, his busy tongue lick lick licking, as if his own life depended on his industry. Nat, looking in on them, gave a mumble-mouthed grin, and went to claim a drink for himself. He found Liz lying back in the cushioned wicker chair, watching firelight flicker on the horse brasses and wink on the empty saddle racks. The hunter's saddle was tossed on the floor. She ought to pick it up. And the stirrups not run up either. Joe would have something to say.

'You ought to see lil owd cat and owd bull,' Nat said, as he poured himself a mug of steaming brew, and held it between his crabby fingers to warm his hands. He blew on the hot liquid, and drank, sucking noisily, sounding like a small pig.

'That's good, missus.'

He looked at her, his blue-grey eyes frankly curious. Not local, Mis' Liz wasn't; came from the Lakes, they said. Be a change for her in this soft country, Cheshire country, farming country. Good country and good rich earth for a man to grow crops, and lush green meadow grass to fatten the cattle, and spreading great trees, all one big park, Cheshire was, not like the Lakes.

He had been there once, on his bicycle, when he wasn't much more than a lad. Bleak fells, grey, and stretching for miles, with nobbut a bird or two to break the vast spaces. And mountains steepening into the sky. And rocks.

48

Not like home, it hadn't been, though the lakes were good to look at, stretching for a mile or more, not like the meres. Colemere and Pickmere and Ellesmere, now they were right pretty with their wooded banks, but cosy, not grand like Coniston and Windermere. Must be a big change to come and live here.

'You like Petley Green?' he asked Liz.

She turned her head and looked at him, considering. Petley Green was a small place, a scatter of farmhouses, the two village shops, one a greengrocer with a nursery garden attached, the other post office and chemist and general store, selling everything under the sun, even farm implements. The old Norman church still watched over the village green.

She nodded, too tired to open her mouth.

'Be a big change after the Lakes,' Nat said, tentative, seeking information.

Liz did not notice.

'A big change,' she agreed and Nat relaxed, satisfied. So it was true, after all. He liked to know, to pigeonhole people, to keep everything tidy inside his mind.

'You want to get a horse,' he said suddenly, looking at the empty saddle racks. 'You want to get a lot of horses. Taught riding, didn't you, before you was wed, or so they say?' he added hastily, suddenly afraid she might resent his questioning.

Liz refilled her own mug, and sat sipping, looking into the flames. She had added a log to the fire and it blazed merrily. She kicked it into sparkling life with her foot.

'I used to teach in a riding school. It was fun,' she said, remembering. Not only good days, but bad days, getting up in the cold of an icy dawn, breaking the ice on the buckets, eating lumpy porridge in the cheerless kitchen and then out to the stables and the horses' steaming breath and the stamp and clatter of hooves, and the feel of the ice-cold tin measure in numb hands. That was where she met Joe, who used to come riding when he was on holiday in the Lake District.

Grooming till she glowed as well as the horse. After-noons spent polishing the tack, the sticky feel of saddle soap, the chatter and the laughter as each girl discussed her latest boy friend, and the pupils she had had that afternoon. Fat girls, with hands that grabbed at the reins and tore at the horses' mouths; and bodies that lumped like suet in the saddle; thin girls, some with hard hands, and some with firm hands, some that rode as if they and the horse belonged, and others that were insensate sacks. It had been fun, she thought regretfully.

'You could start a riding school here. Got room, and it would soon pay its way,' Nat said. It was something he had often thought about, watching the lasses jumping their horses on the telly.

'Here?' Liz stared at him, astounded.

Nat nodded, and pulled his old pipe from his pocket, and filled it, puffing rank smoke into the room. Midge, who was lying on the hearthrug, stalked out of the smoke cloud and Nat laughed at the cat. She sat up, eyeing him, indignant, gave herself a quick wash, her head over one shoulder, and then settled again under Liz's chair. She was not a lap cat, she hated being nursed and swore at anyone who tried to lift her against her will.

'Here,' Nat repeated. 'Got room. Stables for twelve horses out there. Only need a bit of doing up. White-wash and scrubbing. Me and Lew could do that fer you. Used to work with horses, when there was six big fellers up here at Wayman's. Three Shires, two Clydesdales, and a Suffolk Punch. Weren't no older than young Lew in them days.'

'Lovely horses,' Liz said sleepily, thinking of the massive beasts pulling the plough shares, turning the furrows, plodding through the morning.

'Got room for a baker's dozen. And plenty of kids these days want to learn to ride. Any number in the village. And two big-towns in driving distance. Only twenty minutes from Glassford, and about forty from Lingsell. Go into Lingsell and you'll see bags of kids there, and there's kids riding ponies all over the country. New hobby, they call it. Did it when I were nobbut a lad, everybody did.'

Liz sat up, her eyes alert. It was true, she thought, there were plenty of youngsters wanting to learn, like the Fenton children. Paul Fenton had often wished there was a riding school nearby. It had never occurred to her to put her old skill to use. She could fit it in with the farm. Advertise in the two big towns. And take people hacking. It was quiet enough in the lanes, not on a direct route to anywhere.

'You could take folk hunting,' Nat added. He liked the Hunt, and waited for each Meet, getting tips for holding the horses' heads while the riders talked to one another inside the Wheatsheaf over a pint at the end of the day. Helped with the horse boxes too and to rub the tired beasts down. Like old times, it was, when there were none of these beastly engines about. Nasty smelly things, engines.

'Hunting?'

'Not agin it, are yer?' Nat asked, his voice contemptuous.

'I suppose not, not the ride and the chase, anyway,' Liz said, remembering the old thrill of following the foot hounds at home, though glad when they failed to kill.

'All this sentimentality,' Nat said, puffing between words. He gesticulated suddenly with his pipe stem. 'And what about owd fox? You'd think he were an innercent, wouldn't yer? Poor owd fox, chased by hounds and killed. What a way to go. Well, it's quick, isn't it. Not like a fox I found way back, starved to death, from a shot in the shoulder, and gangrene in his leg. Dropped off, it had, and him all bone and a mite of mangy fur.'

Liz shuddered.

'And what about the rabbits? Suppose they don't feel a thing, run down by owd fox and torn apart by him? Folks don't stop to think; don't think of rabbits and hares and birds, ducks and hens and such, and lambs too, owd killer has taken in his life. Oh no. Just think of a pretty furry thing, cuddly cubs and all, and one chase, one death, and him with a life behind him of daily kills. It don't make sense.'

'People often don't make sense,' Liz said, yawning, her mind on the bull. Three hours ago she had been hoping he'd die, before he killed her or Joe or some complete stranger ... or Lew. And now here she was praying he would live and that Joe would never find out she hadn't renewed that damned insurance. She'd do it first thing.

'Better go or be milking time,' Nat said, struggling from the chair.

Liz walked heavily upstairs, her mind on the possibility of buying more horses and teaching riding. The thought of it exhilarated her. She called good-bye to Nat but he was already outside, watching the men come from the bull-pen. He glanced over the half door and down into the straw. The bull was lying down, his breathing heavy. The cat was curled on the animal's back. Casey gazed at Nat with slit green eyes, and purred loudly. The bull lifted his head and twisted it to look at the cat. His tongue licked the sleek fur and Casey purred even more loudly.

52

'He'll do,' Ken Lewis said.

He looked even bigger than his six foot three beside Nat, topping him by over a foot, too slender for his height, his dark skinned face angular, outlined by high cheekbones, and with strangely thick lips at which his tongue teased frequently, the tip flittering in and out, snakelike.

'I'll come back in a few hours,' he added. 'But there's nothing to worry about, now. He's a strong beast and we got to him in time.'

Liz heard the words through the window and sang a small hymn of praise as she undressed. When Joe came up to crawl into bed for a brief three hours she was asleep, and he did not disturb her as he crept in beside her.

Before he turned out the light he heard a small soft sigh. He put down his hand, and Tich crawled from beneath the bed and licked his master, and then curled himself on the rug with his head on Joe's slipper, and lapsed into small canine snores that lulled Joe to sleep, so that soon the room was quiet except for the sound of breathing, and the soft creaking tick of the electric clock.

CHAPTER FIVE

THE bull recovered fast. He was a strong beast.

Casey learned to explore in the long summer days, finding out more about life. Most of his days were the same – days of small adventure and deep pleasure, hours crowded with hunting food and the long sleeps so necessary for all cats.

His world was a strange world, entirely peopled by giants. He divided it for his own benefit into his own giants, who would help him when he was in difficulties, feed him, or make him feel better if he were hurt or ill, and alien giants who were unpredictable. The smaller ones had hands that hurt, that pulled and clutched and tried to pick him up, pinching him and bruising him. He learned to run when he saw them. There were larger strangers with loud voices and uncouth ways, and one in particular, the cowman from down the road, stinking abominably, who, if he passed the farm and saw a cat lurking, lashed out with a heavy boot. Casey learned to hide from him too, and watch, ears flattened, swearing under his breath, until he had gone away again.

There were four legged giants, and they too had their ways. He and Starlight observed a tacit truce, and the stallion did not mind the cat so long as he confined his visit to the stable to sitting on the half door and did not venture inside. There were the cows. Some of them would turn towards him with lowered heads and kick if he came too near. Others tolerated him, and Cherry always spoke to him, lowing a welcome as he trod, soft-footed, through the dew wet grass, and he answered her with his throaty greeting, delighted to be noticed, weaving his sinuous body around her legs.

He loved the wet morning fields. The bull was his, his special property, a creature that welcomed him vociferously, that warmed him on cold nights, that looked anxiously for his coming, but when the first light glinted on the horizon, and Joe Wayman, yawning, opened the half door and fed the great beast and then went to fetch the cows for milking, Casey streaked into the silent fields, fields that belonged to him alone until people awoke.

The grass was long, so his was perennial adventure, unable to see far beyond his small black nose. His routine was unvarying. Over the half door and across the cobbles, keeping to the fence, unwilling, ever, to trust himself in wide open spaces. Long-forgotten ancestral instincts told him there was danger in the open, though what, he did not know. The fear was too great to allow even a bold and curious cat to break the rules built into him.

One summer day was more adventurous than usual. Beyond the fence, over which he leaped, was a ditch, and here was safety. He kept to its shelter, prowling, untamed jungle beastie, through the hedgebottom plants, the long tangling brambles, the high white kex that the children called mother-die, unluckier than may-blossom if brought into the house; brushing aside foxglove and dandelion and long stemmed buttercups. There were thistles that pricked his paws, and nettles through which he crept unscathed, his thick fur a protection.

Dew soaked his coat. The wind brought enticement.

55

He sat to savour it, ears cocked. The world above mocked him, as the birds woke to greet the day, thrush and sparrow, starling and blackbird, the noisy insistent cuckoo cry, and the soft maddening murmur of doves. Birds crowded on bush and tree, and a moorhen ran, head nid-nodding, through the grass towards the pond in the field corner.

Scent of rat and mouse and weasel. Scent of stoat and fox-scent and mole-scent. Aftermath of badger, and of scurrying squirrel. Rabbit and hare, and goose and duck and chicken; the trace of a passing dog, a stranger to the farm. The scent left by Tich on his own explorations, familiar and warming. Tich was a special crony.

Sound of bird and of brumming bee. Sound of water, rushing through a field drain, or wind, hissing in the grasses, bowing the long stems in wave after wave of submission, teasing a length of straw. Casey, seeing the straw, pounced, and then froze again, statuesque, sitting, listening, his cocked ear aware of soft squeaks from the long grass, his nose collecting the exciting pungent smell of mouse.

The stems moved. Casey put out his paw, and a moment later the victim, aware of the hunter, was running desperately through the miniature jungle that surrounded his home. Through grass stem and clover, bending the dandelions, dipping through the tussocks, dodging the new growth of prickly furze. Through the jungle atmosphere too, for the sun was already warm, the dew evaporating, and down among the verdure was a humid, fetid atmosphere that no one walking above would recognize. The mouse, struggling among spiky grass stems, knew panic, a panic that was reinforced as the cat's huge paw struck down at him, knocking him silly.

Casey was hungry. He played for only a few moments with his victim before he tired and stopped to feed. Then he investigated his world further. Beyond him, the grass moved again. He paused, one paw uplifted and curled, and then sat, seeing, for the first time in his life, a strange long tailed bird that bobbed its head as it walked arrogant with pride. Casey watched it browsing in the meadow. He toyed with the idea of stalking and catching it, but its voice was loud and harsh, and it was bigger than he was. He changed his mind, and turned his back, immediately blotting the pheasant from his memory.

A mole, running below the surface, so close that the earth heaved, attracted him next. He reached out a paw, but caught nothing, and stared, bewildered, at the ripple in the ground. He began to circle the field, keeping close to the hedge, commenting loudly as he went.

Joe, bringing the cows back to pasture, could hear the cat's persistent voice, and wondered if it were pleasure or plaint that made him talk to himself all the time. One thing, he thought, as he latched the gate, and gave Cherry the pat which she always demanded, with pushing head against his shoulder, no one could lose Casey, not while he kept up such a din. It was a miracle that he ever caught anything. Hear him a mile away. No sense in the animal.

Casey explored further. He sniffed delightedly at rabbit holes in the bank of the pond, his tail erect and interested, every sense alert. He grumbled noisily when he put his paw in a cow's hoofmark, filled with water after a night of mizzling rain. He chased the moorhen and lost her when she ran squawking into a bramble thicket. He stood on hind legs against the gnarled centuries-old oak and sharpened his claws vigorously, his expression blissful, his eyes half-closed, gaining untold satisfaction from the act. The bark was scored from this daily exercise.

He jumped to the rotting trunk of a fallen tree, now in

full sunshine, and stretched, front legs, hind legs. He sat, eyes almost shut, head lifted to the sun, and his raucous purr caused a nearby bird to call sharply an alarm note that was echoed over and over all through the coppice. Cat. Cat. Cat. The birds maintained this persistent warning so that Liz was always aware of the farm cats and their whereabouts. The danger signal sounded from garden, hedge, field, or haystack, and any cat coming from afar was heralded by the bird noise, growing in intensity as the animal came nearer to the house. The birds seemed to know that the dogs did not presage danger.

Casey loved the sun. He stretched himself along the tree trunk, one paw hanging down on each side of it, his head extended, so that the bark was rough under his chin. His hind legs curled beneath him, his tail swishing gently, not in anger, but in small pleasure. A trait that he inherited from his father, for Tartar also swung his tail gently when he was pleased, and lashed it furiously in his sudden rages.

That morning one of the beagles at the kennels found a way out under the wire. Crazy with freedom, he chased along the lane, turned into a field, hunted rabbit scent along the edge of the ditch, along the line of a drain, through the hedgebottom, along the ditch across the clover field, and ended, panting, glorying in his escape from kennels and people who expected obedience, within ten yards of Casey, who was stretched out, and more than half asleep.

Luckily for Casey, the beagle barked. The cat woke and fled in a single movement that took him along the margin of the pond and into the oak tree. There he sped into the branches and swore in lusty anger, while the beagle stood on his hind legs against the tree and barked back at the cat. Casey had never been treated so in all his short life.

The Wayman's dogs all accepted cats and never barked at them unless they were strangers and then Midge and Casey joined the dogs in the common task of routing the intruder.

Unluckily for Casey, the barn owl was roosting in the tree. He did not like the uproar. He hooted, almost in Casey's ear, and Casey, startled, slipped and fell, landing with difficulty on all four paws.

The beagle dashed into the chase. Casey fled. He dived across the field and blundered through the hedge, he jumped the ditch, leaped the fence, and skidded across the cobbles, flying between Lew's legs, so that Lew over-balanced and landed, fuming, on the midden, while Casey, seeking immediate sanctuary, bolted through the kitchen door with the beagle still on his track. He jumped to the dresser, knocking down two cups which smashed with a noise that frightened him. On the top shelf he crouched with flattened ears and angry eyes, swearing ever more loudly

'Merciful heaven!' Joe said, racing in from the other side of the far field. He aimed a kick at the dog, which took one look at him and bolted. Casey, his fur on end, his tail five times normal size, wailed loudly. He had been chased for his life, he had been terrified, he wanted comfort.

Joe lifted the cat down, and grunted as sharp claws clung to him. Casey had no intention of being abandoned. Gradually he returned to normal, his fluffed fur lay flat again, and soon he was able to make a small purr. Joe took him and put him in the bull-pen.

Casey climbed on to the half door, and then on to the bull's head. Here he sat, and all the time that they went about their duties in the yard, Lew and Joe could hear the cat's constant conversation, for all the world as if he were telling the bull the whole of his morning's adventure.

'Daft lil owd cat,' Lew said, scratching the old Middle-white boar on his fat neck. 'Fair owd caution, in't he?'

There were only two occasions on which Casey prowled at night. Usually Joe shut him in the bull-pen. When he forgot, Casey reminded him, long after midnight, yowling desperately, waking the chickens to terrified idiot clamour, waking the dogs to sudden fury, waking the bull to lowing competition, asking for Casey to be allowed to visit him and comfort him, while the cows, disturbed by the din, called from the meadow, and Joe and Liz cursed at the interruption to their sleep.

The first time that this happened was early dusk. Casey had been crouched in the haystack watching the swallows skitter in the yard, darting only a few inches from the ground.

He was fascinated by the dark. He came out into the yard when the swallows had gone to roost and the last bats had also flittered homewards to the crannies in the barn and the vast oak in the cattle field.

Casey sniffed the night and stared at the darkness. Cow tang and sheep tang. Shadow of a cruising owl. It flew to the barn roof and sat, swivel head twisting, knowing that here was rat and mouse.

The owl saw him and swooped. Casey heard the feather flight, saw the shadow bulk, felt the talon that tore at his shoulder, and he was down the post and across the yard with his heart thudding so loudly that it deafened him. Paws trembling, fur fluffing, he fled into the shelter of the barn among the hay bales, where he crouched and shook until the hooting owl mourned away into the distance, and he crept out, and shrieked to Liz and Joe to come and let him in, in to the dark safety and the warm company of his favourite, old Sultan.

Joe, coming down, bad-tempered, pyjama clad, lifted the cat, feeling every sinew tense with fear, feeling terrified claws dig deep into his neck, feeling the uneasy fur harsh, on end, seeing the wildness in the sea-green eyes.

'Poor old fellow,' he said, his voice soothing, aware that some dire danger had threatened Casey, but unaware of its source. Slowly the cat's fur flattened and his ears came erect again, and panic died in Casey's eyes. Only the tip of his tail was bottle-brushed when Joe opened the pen and put him inside. Long after the farmer had huddled against Liz to warm his shivering body he heard the cat relaying his adventure, and the bull's rumble question-and-answer-sounding, a fantasy that made him grin in the darkness.

'Damn funny lil owd cat,' he thought in Lew's words, and slept the sleep he deserved.

Casey's second nocturnal adventure was much more alarming. This night was hot, thunder stifling, clouds brooding low, lightning flicker-flashing, and a distant continuous reverberating giant rumble that made the creatures restless in stalls and pens and chicken house and kennels. The bull lowed constantly and the pen was oven-warm and fetid and Joe left the door half open to let in some night air, and left the dogs on guard, though goodness knew that anyone who tried to steal a bull would suffer for their sins in no small measure.

The night called. The grass moved enticingly, telling of hidden mouse and rabbit. Urgent with the hungry hunting goad, Casey crept, stiff-legged, around the edge of the yard, so close to the fence that he brushed it. He scanned the posts for owls, but none were near. He saw a tantalizing shadow in the grass, a sudden movement as a rabbit scented him and bounded for its burrow, small white fluff scut prominent when it leaped, ears listening, eyes starting, nose telling of ever-closer danger, the cat smell, the scare smell, filling his nostrils till he ran panic-mad, in a small circle, and turned towards the cat and in an ecstasy of terror, humped forwards, hurling his body at the prowling beast that followed him on quicksilver light paws.

Casey, startled, jumped aside, and the rabbit turned and fled, legs thumping the ground, alerting the vixen that lay in the hollow. She had five mouths to feed and no dog fox to help her. Her ears pricked, and she sat, wary-wild, eyes searching, nose begging the wind to tell her where this night's meal was hiding. Saliva dripped from her lips, and she licked her chops, the milk not dry in her, the youngsters draining her strength, the mother-need clamouring for sustenance.

She saw the rabbit as he jumped in one last frantic movement and reached his burrow. She saw Casey bound, and stand, bewildered by the sudden disappearance of his victim. Casey was rabbit coloured, furry, food-smell. She was a small young vixen and had never encountered a cat before. Her swift run and sudden pounce brought her within feet of Casey, but he had glimpsed her flashing body, caught the rank scent of her and jumped backwards, landing on his feet, fluffing his fur, within inches of the wire fence.

He had two methods of defence, methods which might save him from fighting. The vixen to him was huge. Her foul smell choked him. His fur lifted, until he was five times cat size, enlarged and angered, ears flattened on his small head. The vixen waited, watching him, uneasy. She was hungry but this was a beast outside her experience.

Casey used his second line of defence. He sang his battle cry, louder and louder, fiercer and fiercer, roaring to a crescendo of fury, the yell of an enraged Siamese, a yell that brought Joe running and the dogs headlong, barking, as the vixen, not to be baulked of food, sprang.

Casey rolled on to his back. His long-clawed front legs savaged her face, raking, tearing, lashing for eyes and jaw, vulnerable and easy. His long feline teeth met through her shoulder pad. His hind legs, side by side, raked, claws out, at her belly, as she twisted and tried for a hold. She had only a moment, before Tich came across the field, having dug his frenzied way under the wire fence, and the shelties ran and tore and bit any part of the fox that they could find unguarded.

The vixen released the cat, and fled, over the field and along a furrow, through the cattle, and into the far field, and Joe's gun sent an angry bark after her, the shot spitting into the ground not ten feet behind her flying heels. She ran until she was breathless, and fed on frogs and beetles, and returned to her nursing young with scratches that would hurt her for weeks, and an aversion to cats that would last her a lifetime.

The angry crack of the gun sent one of the shelties flying, gunshy, to the haystack, sent Casey pell mell, away from the din, and back to the bull-pen, where he crouched in the straw, and every now and then released his feelings in a reminiscent cussing that made the bull peer at him suspiciously, as if doubtful whether the cat might not attack him too. It was a long time before Casey settled.

He had a bite on one leg and another on his shoulder, he needed careful grooming, in every part and corner of him, and the slow working of his busy tongue soothed him. He washed every inch devotedly, licking at the two sore places over and over, and then fell to washing the bull, until his tongue tired and his eyes closed and he stretched out against the giant animal.

Sultan rested his head on the ground near the cat. The cat slept, and soon the bull slept too, his face against the small body, his ears alert for any movement that would betray Casey's departure and startle him to lonely forlornness again. There were three hours left to cockcrow.

CHAPTER SIX

IT had been a bad week.

Three days before two strange pigs had come bolting into the kitchen out of the blue. Half a day and three phone calls later a neighbouring farmer arrived with a trailer to collect them and apologize, and share a cup of coffee, and air his own complaints about form-filling and Government policies. The day's chores were completed at the double.

The previous night Starlight had let himself out of the stable and a fine time they had had catching the stallion, who wanted to roll in the meadow, and savour his freedom. He could not be left in the field as fences were no obstacle and the local police took a jaundiced view of a large black stallion trotting serenely alone down the centre of the road towards the major road at the end of the lane, which was only three miles from the M6 motorway. Get him on there. . . .

Liz, scalding churns, found herself hoping devoutly that nothing more would go wrong with this particular day. She was tired and every bone in her body ached, after chasing Starlight and trying to control him by herself. He was much too powerful, and she and Nat and Lew took all their time to get him back to the stable, where he pawed angrily at the ground and spent the evening in rank bad temper, neighing shrilly, his high stallion scream noisy and impatient, whenever anyone crossed the yard. Joe, who had been to the Beast Sale and come back disappointed because he had been outbidden for three Jersey heifers, and a little mare he wanted for Liz, went to console the animal, but Starlight would have none of him. Luckily, Lew passed them later that night, wandering home from the river, with a trout tucked under his shirt, and hearing the din, went in to offer his own comfort. Before long his caressing fingers had soothed away annoyance, and he groomed the beast, and gave him a handful of carrots, and went across to the kitchen to say good night to Liz and Joe.

'I don't know what we'd do without you, Lew,' Liz said, and meant it. Lew was invaluable. He seemed to think like an animal, and could control any of the beasts on the farm, sensitive at once to their needs and feelings.

Lew grinned and blushed, and backed away awkwardly, embarrassed by the compliment, but he was singing to himself as he went down the lane.

'Folk don't know half there is to know about Lew,' Liz said, more than grateful for his help and willingness and the cheerful way in which he worked as hard as anyone, and never thought to grumble.

She was thinking of him now, as she hefted the churns, and then hosed down the dairy. He had come to her in enormous distress, just before milking. One of the cows had dropped dead without warning. She had rung Ken Lewis and arranged for a post mortem, and asked him to contact the knacker. He, arriving in a hurry, took one look at the cow and searched the field carefully. By then all the other cows were in the yard or in the milking parlour.

He found what he was looking for in a corner under

66

the hedge. They had had visitors in the night, who had used the field as a dumping place. There was an old tyre, a pram wheel, a cot mattress, and a sack of white powder, which had spilled over the grass. White tracks away from it showed where the cows had walked.

'Looks like rat poison,' Ken said, putting the powder on his fingers and sniffing.

'I wish to heaven people would learn to behave properly,' Liz said furiously. 'They're always dumping their rubbish in our fields. Last week someone chucked an old bicycle and a child's pram into the pond. It took Lew half the morning to fish it out and make sure there wasn't any broken glass there as well. That's the cattle's drinking pool, but nobody thinks of that.'

'Penalty of the affluent society,' Ken said morosely. 'More junk than they know what to do with, so they bring it out here. You'll never know who killed your cow for you. I'd like to break his neck,' he added viciously.

'So would I,' Liz said. 'I'll get the insurance for her, but she was in calf. And that won't get made up. And we'll probably buy in a heifer, and not a milker, so we've lost her milk too. And she was a good milker. Nice beast too, poor old Poll.'

She left the men to deal with the body. Always some beast dying on a farm. You got used to it, but you always minded, though some you minded more than others. She would never give another thought to Sultan if he died. Beastly animal. He seemed quieter after his long immersion, but he still glowered at her from his pen whenever she crossed the yard, and she was always conscious of his pawing hoof, and the way he banged his horns against the concrete wall. Sometimes his weird lowing made the place hideous for hours. She was always thankful when his pen was safely cleaned, even though the yoke held his body firmly, so that Lew could work safely around him. It did not hold his hooves.

She turned to see Joe walking morosely towards the Land-Rover. He had put the cattle in the second field, which was earmarked for hay. They would lose the whole crop from those acres, thanks to their night-time visitor, who probably only thought he was getting rid of un-wanted rubbish and doing no more harm than making the place untidy. She set her lips. Take a while to get that field clean again, and they were short of decent grazing land.

As Joe climbed in the Land-Rover, Bennie and Tich started barking. Tich, instead of jumping in after his master, stood in front of the vehicle, his small body con-torted with the need to make himself understood. Bennie, who only barked at intruders, and was trained to perfect discipline, was, most unusually, ignoring Joe's yells for silence, and making even more noise. Both dogs had their eyes firmly fixed on their master's face.

Liz went to see what was wrong. Midge and Tartar were agitated too, and Tartar added his own noise to the din, which was becoming deafening. Midge's small anxi-ous mew was lost in the uproar.

She went to the dogs. Joe was standing staring at them completely at a loss. There seemed no sense to their noise. Bennie pushed his nose urgently against Liz's leg. She looked about her. The Land-Rover stood in a patch of brilliant sunlight. There was nothing else to be seen.

'Quiet!' Joe roared at the top of his voice.

The dogs quieted, but continued to look at him un-happily. Tartar took no notice. No one was going to dic-tate to a cat, especially to a Siamese cat. He yowled loudly.

A small voice answered him sleepily.

'My God!' said Joe.

He bent forward to look, and Liz bent with him. Casey was stretched luxuriously on the Land-Rover wheel, draped along the tyre under the wheel arch, basking in the sunlight, his body relaxed and blissful, his paws hanging loose.

He yawned at them, his small mouth scarlet, his small tongue curled. His white pointed teeth glistened. He stretched himself, greeted them with fervour, and then, as Liz lifted him, with a tremendous throbbing purr. He rubbed his head against her face, curled his paws against her neck, and settled to sleep again. Liz blinked. If the Land-Rover had started . . .

'He might have jumped down when he heard the engine,' Joe said, but his voice was uncertain. He patted the dogs. 'Good fellers then. Good dogs.'

Bennie wagged a vigorously enthusiastic tail and went back to lie in the shade cast by the stables. It was a hot day, and every movement made him pant. He stretched out on the cool cobbles and lay with his nose between his paws, his ears, half-cocked, and his eyes on the gate. No strangers would ever get the better of Bennie.

Tich, now satisfied, jumped into the Land-Rover. Joe leaned out and grinned to Liz.

'Born to trouble,' he said. 'One thing, nothing else can go wrong today. I should think we've had more than our share. Damn the fellow that chucked that poison on my field. I wish I could get hold of him and rub his nose in it.'

Liz watched the Land-Rover turn out into the lane. She fastened the gate, and went slowly back to the house. It was too hot to breathe. The sky, in spite of the heat, was sullen, brooding above the farm. There would be a storm before the night was out and that would mean fun. Starlight was terrified of thunder and it upset the bull, so that he was both noisy and restless.

She put Casey down and he sauntered round the yard, and finally stretched himself again in the sunshine. It was too hot for him to get into further trouble, she decided, going into the shady house, where the stone walls and stone floors made a cool haven. She began to make a salad, wandering in and out of the kitchen, one eye on the clock and the other on the animals. Tartar and Midge were lying stretched luxuriously, side by side, in the shade cast by the well roof. The cover was off the well – the water had been smelling stagnant. The two big cats were old enough to know that the sun was too hot. She wondered if cats could get sunstroke, wondered if she should move Casey into the shade, and then left him. He would have to learn for himself.

The brooding thunder was unsettling. Liz felt restless and uneasy all morning. Soon the sun had gone, and the sky was completely overcast, louring banks of heavy cloud massing sulphurous on the horizon, black and heavy with rain, and threatening. Twice sheet lightning flashed across the sky. Midge and Tartar had gone to lie by the haystack, sheltered by the big barn roof. Casey was nowhere to be seen.

Had she looked, Liz would have soon found him. Casey had discovered enchantment. It lay in a feather. A long goose feather had been shed that morning. He tapped it with an experimental paw, and it flicked away from him, falling gently. He mouthed it curiously. It tasted of bird; the taste was rich and exciting, but unsatisfying. He flung his head up, and the feather tossed above him for a moment and then floated towards the ground. He darted towards it and sprang, teasing it with mouth and paws.

The game had endless possibilities. He stood on his hind legs and tossed the feather and caught it. He pounced and bounced and dived, he twisted and danced, and teased it. He flicked it with a paw, tossing it, now broken and dirty, in the air, where it was just heavy enough to rise above his head before falling again.

The wind that came before the storm took the feather and blew it playfully along the cobbles. Casey fled after it, darted, sprang and caught it with both front paws. He growled at it, menacing it, daring it to defy him. He picked it up in his mouth, flung it above his head, pounced on all four legs, leaping high, to spring down on it, came to the ground, twisted violently to grab the feather which had slipped away from him, jumped again as it drifted enticingly in front of his nose . . . and fell. There was nothing whatever beneath him. The liberated feather floated on the wind, out of his reach, and was gone.

There was only darkness. He saw it as he dropped, having leaped the brickwork of the well in his last jump and missed his footing. He saw the world above him narrow to a circle of light, shadowed by the well roof and the handle of the swinging bucket. He saw the sky grow small and far away and he smelled a strangeness that choked and nauseated him.

The water was beneath him, and a moment later he was in it, with a splash that terrified him. He was sinking, but his instinct for life took over, so that he soon surfaced, and paddled frantically, crying to people to come and help.

This time, nobody heard. Casey was on his own.

He hated water. His fur clung to his body and his mouth was full of water. He swallowed the beastly stuff in frantic fear and submerged again. He came up beside the brick wall and scrabbled desperately with his paws. His claws found purchase and he pulled himself slowly out of the icy wetness and crawled laboriously towards the light.

The light was miles away. His paws slithered on damp green slime. Moss cloaked the brickwork, which was old and uneven. Casey began to slip. Even as he slipped Joe came back into the yard in the Land-Rover, and the first grumbles of thunder sounded in the sky.

Casey did not like thunder. He had never heard it so noisy before in his short life, nor seen anything quite like the brilliance that suddenly flashed over the top of the well, hurting his eyes. He yowled at the top of his voice, wild with terror. He reached out a frenzied paw, fighting for better purchase, and encountered a rough wide pipe. It gave him shelter from the weird light that danced over the sky, sheeting across it time and time again in successive waves, so that the world was momentarily incandescent, and after the light came the rolling drum-peals, echoing in that confined space so that Casey added blind terror to his other woes. He crouched in the pipe, shivering and calling.

This time his cries were heard. Joe, shutting the half doors on the bull and the stallion so that they could not see the lightning, heard the cat, and, a few moments later, identified the place from which the yowls were coming. He cursed fluently and ran for the ladder, which he put into the well, and began to climb down. Liz, hearing him shout, came too and peered at him from above, anxious for both of them.

'Water's not more than two feet deep,' Joe called up to her. 'Enough to drown Casey, but no need to worry about me.'

His voice echoed eerily from the brickwork, and was reinforced by a blazing flash and a thunder roll that sent Casey scuttering up the pipe out of reach of the being that made such weirdly terrifying noises at him. Although he was shivering with cold he panted in terror, and Joe, reaching an arm into the pipe, could not get near him.

'Come on, stupid,' he said softly, but the pipe took the sound and built it into sinister sibilants and unspeakable inhuman whistles, and Casey retreated even farther.

'Try pouring water down the pipe from the bathroom window and see if you can flush him down,' Joe called up to Liz. 'He's in the pipe that runs from the gutter, luckily. Not the one that leads to the sewer.'

The ensuing flood soaked Joe, but Casey only anchored himself against the rough glazing, and cried pitifully and remained immobile, his body flattened, his paws outstretched, trying to keep his purchase on this suddenly cold and bitter cruel world. An echo of thunder sent him even higher up the pipe, and deafened Joe who swore viciously as wind drove the sudden thunderpour into the well and down his neck. He was up to the knees in water, and feeling more and more that this was fool's play.

His temper, already trigger-haired because of the dead cow, vanished completely.

'Casey!'

It was a lion roar, echoing and resounding, and Casey went upwards and away, leaving Joe to wonder how in the world they could ever get the cat out of his dark and damp retreat. Lucky the pipe was very wide. He'd have air. But he doubted if even the firemen would know how to rescue the silly animal and upon his soul, he didn't. Needed something to push in and pull the cat out, but what? That was the problem.

Liz came back with a plate of fish. Casey loved fish, but even as Joe put it in the pipe opening there was the crack of final doom, and a fire flash dropped from the sky

73

and hit the old oak in the far field. The oak split with the noise of devils in a haunting army, the thunder rolled again and again, deafening Joe, and Casey vanished, and crouched, paralysed with fear, in a bend in the pipe, out of the reach of the bewildering and completely inexplicable light that kept illuminating the body of the well.

Joe tied a pice of netting over the end of the pipe so that the cat could not fall back into the water. He climbed back to the yard again, and turned to face Lew who was standing leaking water from every garment, his face scarlet with wind, but as always, grinning.

'Us got ketched in a dumberdash,' he said, as they squelched towards the farmhouse, both as wet as if they had jumped into the river.

'Indeed, us did,' Joe agreed, falling into Lew's idiom, which always pleased him. They stood and their clothes made wide pools on the scullery floor, and Liz brought towels and a change for both of them, and listened to the driving rain which the wind hurled at the windows, and the protesting trees, and the peal and echo of thunder. The storm was receding, and the lightning flickered in the distance now, but she could not help thinking of the cat, crouching in the dark wet pipe, unable to understand at all what had happened to his safe world where people could always be relied upon to help him.

She began to cook the supper. The afternoon had vanished while they were trying to rescue Casey. Lew and Joe went off with raincoats over their heads to fetch the cows for milking, and salad was no good for them now, on a night like this. She began to cook chips, and found that Joe had brought fish home for next day with him, so she cooked that too.

Casey was lured towards the smell. His mouth filled with saliva, drooling at the thought of soft flaked fish,

74

tender on his tongue, and milk, rich and creamy and fresh from the cow and infinitely satisfying. Joe always took off a bucketful for the cats and dogs and any young animals that might be bottle fed and the cats and dogs helped themselves, each one coming to the bucket to take his own share. Casey had to stand on his hind legs to reach inside, even when it was full. And then he had to reach in his paw and lick that for he was still too small to get his head down and lap. Only Bennie could do this with ease. Midge and Tartar both perched on the edge of the bucket, but Casey had once overbalanced and had a bath of milk and he was not anxious to repeat the experience. The bucket would be filling now. The storm had died away and he could hear the cattle milling in the yard. Milking time, and eating time, and fish cooking and he was not there.

People had failed him. It was entirely up to him. He began to use his claws to ease himself up, inch by slow inch, along the pipe, slimy with years of dripping from the gutters, noisome with the smell of enclosed space, and the stagnant water in the well, which was only used in emergencies for the cattle. The air was rancid and bitter and Casey choked as he breathed. Now and again he paused for breath, and uttered miserable wails that were completely inaudible outside the well and so distorted by the pipe that his own yowls frightened him.

Long minutes dragged by as he hauled himself on. The cattle went back to the sodden fields and stood miserably, turning away from the rain, huddling for comfort, now and then licking one another in friendship, a warm tongue being reassuring as a mother's affection. One of the cows coughed. Another lowed, and the well magnified their breathing and their noise so that they sounded close. Bats came out and flitted in the still air. The storm had gone, and left behind a new-washed world, and a sky that was pure as the colour of a larkshell and fading to dusk. Casey continued to climb. The pipe led from the well and then upward until it came out of the ground and slanted steeply to the second storey gutter. The cat was no longer aware of anything. He was numb with cold, exhausted with effort, oblivious of the smell of food, of thoughts of milk, or warmth, or affection. But he had to go on. He had to get out.

Somewhere below him the bull lowed. It was late and the cat had not come to see him as he always did. Casey's timetable was unvarying. After milking was over the animals were fed, and when he had his own supper he went out to see Sultan. He returned to the kitchen after Liz had washed the dishes and at her bedtime went back to the bull-pen and curled against the bull to sleep until dawn. Then he walked into the mysterious morning, and hunted through the silent fields loving the quiet of day when no human disturbed the peace, and no noises came to baffle or bewilder him. That was the magic moment of his day, and when he had savoured it he slept in the bull-pen until breakfast time.

He heard the bull and braced his small cold body and began to claw his way up again, through an endless darkness, on and on without any hope or any reason, except that downwards led to the water, and that, he knew, did not lead him out of the place into which he had fallen.

Joe, when he had eaten, returned to the well, and Lew came too and called to Casey.

'Hey, lil owd puss, lil owd Casey. Come an' see Lew. Where yer gone to then? Coom on out, no one's goin' to hurt yer. C'm on, lil owd cat, coom to Lew, then.'

Liz called and beat her tocsin. Casey always came running at the sound of a fork banged against his tin plate, appearing from nowhere with tail erect and eyes shining, speeding so fast that he skidded on the cobbles and his long slender legs crossed over one another in their haste and his voice called excitedly as he ran, ending in one splendid yowl as he executed his food and love dance all around the kitchen floor and rubbed against Liz's legs. He would never settle to feed until she had picked him up and stroked him and rubbed her chin against his head, and he had gazed back at her with adoring eyes that were half closed as he looked up at her, blissful because she was noticing him. He was as demonstrative and as much in need of affection as any Siamese, and had inherited all of Tartar's most pronounced characteristics. Casey heard the sound of the fork. He was not going back. He struggled on.

'It's useless,' Joe said at last. 'He must have fallen through the net and drowned, or suffocated in the pipe. Water must be going through after all that rain. I must try and find him somehow. Can't have a dead cat in the pipe or in the well.'

Liz set her lips. Men! No thought for the poor cat at all. She went about the kitchen, tidying up after the day's jobs. She set a match to the logs. It was chilly after the rain. Lew kept them supplied with fine kindling and she soon had a blaze. She stretched out her hands. This was Casey's time, when he came in to see her, and sat, a ball of glossy fur, on her lap, sometimes washing himself vigorously, ending with a lick at her hand, to show that he appreciated her comfort, sometimes curling in a tight ball, purring contentedly, as he slept, somehow giving the evening its crown of leisure. There was nothing quite so companionable and relaxing as a cat upon the hearth-rug. Nothing quite so entertaining as Casey, purring loudly, thanking her for food and drink. Appearing as if by magic whenever she brought liver, so eager to eat that he bit her leg while she was cutting it up for him. Full of life and vigour and curiosity. Dancing with the falling leaves, chasing butterflies, yowling in grief and holding up for her inspection a paw stung by a wasp. Casey had had an eventful life, but it looked as if his last adventure had ended it. Liz could not sit still. She wandered aimlessly round the kitchen, seeing a dancing Casey in every dusky corner.

Finally she gave up and went to bed. Joe had been to the Wheatsheaf and collected suggestions as to how to rescue the cat, and come back with four men all big with ideas, and she suspected, fairly big with beer. She soon tired of them and their laughter, and made the excuse to go up early. She was in her bath when she heard, unbelievingly, the familiar mew, feeble but unmistakable. She jumped out of the water, leaned out of the fanlight at the top of the window and looked upwards. Casey, dirty, draggled, soaked and despairing, looked down at her with incredulous eyes and batted rust from the gutter into her mouth with his agitated paw which was stretching downward, urgent and demanding, towards her.

Liz yelled.

There was a thunder of boots on the cobbles. The men called up to her. Joe, sure that murder was being done, bolted across the yard and stared up at her, as she gestured frantically, clutching a towel to hide her nakedness, irritated by the other men down there, all gawping too. Casey reached towards her, and, afraid that he would fall, she leaned further from the window, holding him back. She could not grip him. He was just out of reach, and only her hand against his chest enabled him to keep his balance.

Joe fetched the ladder and shinned up it hurriedly, grabbed the cat, dropped him through the window, and shot down to the yard again to quieten the bull, who seeing the ladder stretching lengthways beside his pen, as Joe carried it, decided there were creatures abroad in the night that he did not like and began to paw and trample the straw, and then to low his desolation because he had not seen Casey for the whole long day.

Meanwhile Casey had fallen into the bath, his numbed paws unable to balance him.

Into hot water this time. He mewed with rage, and Liz rescued him, laughing, and dried herself hastily while he sat in the washbasin and tried without avail to clean his grimy coat. His small tongue began to ache.

Liz dressed, and then she bathed him. She put water into the basin, took soap, and a thick pad of cotton wool. Indignant, furious, a pathetic bundle of draggled fur and bones, Casey forgot his manners and spat and swore and bit and scratched, never having been so treated in his whole life.

Some time afterwards, rolled in a warm towel in front of a blazing fire, he recovered his temper, and licked Liz's hand in apology while she fluffed his drying fur, and fed him on warm milk laced with brandy, a taste that shocked him and then left him ecstatically warm, so that he curled against Midge and Tich and kneaded the rug with his claws and purred noisily.

Later that night he sat in the yard, watching the moon shine through latticed dark cloud. He watched the trees as they bowed and swayed, played briefly with a twist of twine and then stalked purposefully across the yard.

'Born to trouble,' Joe observed, watching the cat through the window.

Liz watched too. The bull-pen was closed and locked

for the night. Casey yowled. Sultan heard him and answered ecstatic. Casey came back to the bedroom window and yowled again.

'That damned cat,' Joe said, and went downstairs, and outside, and opened up the half-door. Quicker than a darting swallow, Casey was inside, greeting the bull, rubbing against the beast's legs, purring loudly and continuously in a paean of happiness.

The bull was lying down. He pushed his own head against the little cat, licked Casey with a vast red tongue, and then settled himself comfortably as the cat curled up and began to purr even more loudly.

Sultan moved so that his head sheltered the small beast. Joe watched them, and grinned to himself as he shut the half-door and locked the pen again.

'Funny lil owd cat,' he said, once more paraphrasing Lew, as he climbed into bed. 'And darned if that damned bull didn't sound as if he was purring too.'

Liz didn't hear him. It had been a long day, and she was sound asleep. Tich thumped his stump tail to prove that he had heard, and then curled up too.

CHAPTER SEVEN

THE telephone bell, ringing just as milking ended, was an outrage. Liz, who felt as if she had had no sleep at all, answered it, leaving bacon frizzling in the pan.

'Liz!' Jill Fenton's voice was desperate. 'It's Candy . . . she's ill. I don't know what on earth's wrong, and Ken Lewis is out . . . can you come? You might be able to help.'

'I'll be right over,' Liz promised.

She put the bacon on a plate, snatched her thick jacket, dragged a comb through her hair, and rushed out of the kitchen door, cannoning into Joe, who was coming in at an equal speed, ravenous after two hours' work without food.

'Coffee in the pot, bacon on your plate, cook your own eggs. Candy's ill,' Liz said, diving for the Land-Rover. Joe stared blankly at her retreating back and then, as the engine coughed to life, her meaning penetrated.

'Always something,' he said to Midge who had been un-successful in her night's hunting, and was busy being an extra-loving cat, anxious for a handout. Joe put food down for her, and for the dogs, poured his coffee, and sat back to eat in comfort, aware that his breakfast was well-earned. Cattle milked and back in the fields, churns at the gate, yard hosed down, and the bull-pen clean. The bull was thoughtful this morning, and seemed subdued, and Joe had given him extra feed, and grinned as he watched Casey industriously stalking a non-existent mouse, almost under the beast's hooves.

Liz took the Land-Rover to the field where Candy was lying under a tree. Jill and Paul standing helpless beside her. There was no room to park in the lane.

'Thank heaven you've come,' Paul said, looking up unhappily. 'The poor beast's in agony.'

Liz took one look at the pony. She was trying to stand, moving awkwardly and uncomfortably, her head weaving from side to side, uttering low grunts of pain.

'Honestly, Paul!' Liz was exasperated. 'She's foaling. Didn't you know?'

'I never even thought of it,' Jill said. 'Besides, we've had her over nine months and there hasn't been another horse near.'

'Horses take ten months,' Liz said. Her hands were stroking the little beast's neck. 'She'll be all right. This is quite normal. I don't think she should have any trouble. It's not as if it were her first foal.'

'I'll get off.' Paul hated nature in the raw, preferring to forget the harder facts of life. It was pleasanter to imagine that birth was an easy business, even though his wife had tried to tell him differently and always refused to have the third child that he wanted. He thought her selfish, but now, after watching the little mare, he was less certain. Perhaps things weren't so simple, after all.

'She'll have to come to us when she's had it,' Liz said. 'You can't keep the foal outside in this weather. Too much rain. I've got a spare loose-box, and I can get feed for Candy. She'll need an extra nourishing diet.'

'Lew was trying to tell me something the other day,' Jill said. Even at that time of day she was perfectly

82

dressed, her sleek dark hair elegant, her face made up. She had turned her back to the mare, unable to bear the sight of the animal's pain. Liz was stroking the soft muzzle, answering the appeal in the dark brown eyes, giving what comfort she could. Candy accepted it, deriving some relief from the knowledge that she was not alone.

'What's the matter with Candy?'

The children had come headlong, Jane in pyjamas and dressing gown, her slippers dark with dew that soaked them. Her blonde pigtails were half undone. Peter's face was white as he looked at the struggling pony. He had put on his jeans and his jersey was back-to-front. His dark hair was rough, needing a comb.

'Is she going to have to die?' Jane asked, her wide blue eyes anxious.

'She's going to have a baby,' Liz said. 'Why don't you help mummy make her some warm gruel? She'll be hungry.'

The mare heaved her whole body. She struggled suddenly to her feet, and with one convulsive movement the foal was out, lying beside her, while she panted disastrously.

'Go in at once,' Jill said angrily, but the children were on the grass beside the new baby, looking at his slimed coat and the long hanging cord.

'He's sweet,' Jane breathed, absorbed, her hand moving to touch the foal and then drawing back again. 'He's sweet.'

'Candy wants to lick him clean,' Liz said. 'Go in, there's good children. She's coming to stay with us for a little while, but you can come and see her whenever you like.'

The children watched as the pony bent to her son, and began to groom away the membrane that wrapped him.

'She'll be very thirsty,' Liz said, 'and probably hungry too. You can bring her a bucket of water . . . get the chill off it first. Add a little hot water. And she could do with some brandy in her gruel. She'll want food soon,' she added to Jill as the children sped away.

'I wish they hadn't come,' Jill said unhappily. 'That's the last thing I wanted them to see. Heaven knows what effect it will have on unformed minds. It might haunt them for ever.'

'Rubbish!' Liz had no patience with such nonsense. 'They thought it was wonderful, and so do I. If they live in the country they'll see lambs born and calves, and piglets. You can't keep the world from them, and why on earth do you want to? I love watching the calves being born . . . you never know how the cow will react . . . and they are so proud! Look at Candy. She knows she's been clever!'

'I still think it's disgusting. Ugh!' Jill went back to the house, to busy herself with the gruel. She hoped that Paul would sell the pony, and they'd buy the children a gelding. She had never dreamed that this would happen.

Liz took the bucket from the children, and gave it to the little mare. The honey brown pony drank thirstily, gulping every drop, sucking noisily at the last traces so that the children grinned. Jane wanted to touch the foal, to hug him to her, but she did not dare. Candy might not like it, and Candy had proved, on more than one occasion, that when she was displeased, she could kick.

'Eh,' said Lew's awed voice behind Liz. No one had seen him come into the field. 'Eh. Her's clever.' His speech was always broader when he was excited.

He bent to Candy, patting her, stroking her, as pleased as if the foal was his, completely entranced by the small creature. He looked at it, but did not touch. Candy might be jealous. Better to let her be.

'Foal's wick,' he said proudly, as the foal pulled itself up legs tangling absurdly. Within minutes it was nosing at the pony's flanks, ready to suckle.

'What on earth does he mean?' Jill asked, as she handed the gruel pan to Lew.

'Wick means lively,' Liz said, used to Lew's odd words. Some of them were most descriptive. 'You'll get used to country talk in a bit. We've got an urchant in our haystack. And the other day Joe got ketched in a dumberdash, and there's askers in the pond.'

'Meaning?' Candy was busy with the gruel pan, ravenous after the effort of giving birth.

Liz laughed.

'An urchant is a hedgehog. And Joe was caught in a downpour . . . I think dumberdash is a lovely word. And askers are newts.'

'The children bring home some funny words from school,' Jill said. She was happier now that the birth was over and the foal standing, and clean.

'Stay with Candy, will you, Lew?' Liz asked. 'I'll go back for the horse-box.'

'Her's coming to us?' Lew beamed at them. Another beast to care for, another loose-box occupied, and a foal as well.

Liz brought the horse-box into the field. Candy looked at it dubiously. She had only travelled in one once before, and she had hated every minute of it. She nosed her foal, pushing him away from the unfamiliar vehicle, and from Lew.

' 'Twon't hurt yer,' Lew said, cajoling. He held out his hand. 'Come on then, owd Candy. Lew won't let them hurt you.'

Jill looked at him in astonishment. Used to his mono-syllables when she spoke to him, she was startled to hear how vocal he became when he spoke to animals.

'Come along then, Candy, luv. In box wi' ye.'

Candy tossed her mane and arched her neck, and pawed the ground. The foal was standing behind her, struggling to control his legs, which appeared to have a mind of their own, quite separate from his brain. He tottered towards her, leaning against her flank.

'Have to pick the foal oop and take him first,' Lew said. Candy stood foursquare, firm, her hooves planted. There might be ghosts or devils in the dark, or strange hobgob-lins to bedevil her. There might be wild beasts lurking, ready to pounce on her son. There might be men with whips. There was a strange smell, a terrifying smell, for the box had not been cleaned out after carrying pigs home the night before. Not even a pouncing tiger could coax Candy inside. She had never met a pig.

'I'll have to take the children to school,' Jill said.

The sun was bright in a metalled sky. A blackbird sang his praise of the morning in the elm tree at the edge of the field. Tartar sat watching a moving clump of grass, his head on one side, his eyes brilliant with interest, his ears moving to catch the faint intriguing rustles made by the wind. It might be a lurking mouse. He bent an eager head, and sniffed. Candy watched him as suspiciously as she eyed the horse-box.

'Her'll never go,' Lew said.

He moved swiftly and picked up the foal and went into the box with it. Candy neighed her panic and fled up the ramp with thumping hooves. The foal, lying quietly on the floor, too young to know fear, not yet taught about the world by his mother, gazed up at her. Lew slid out fast, aware that Candy could both bite and kick, and under the circumstances, almost certainly would lash out in anger, because he had handled her son. She bent her head to the foal, and he raised his own muzzle to meet hers, his soft warm breath fanning her nostrils. In her joy of him, the outside world was forgotten, and she stood quietly as the door was fastened, and made no protest when the horse-box was jolted out of the field and into the narrow lane, Liz manoeuvring patiently so that she could turn between the high hedges.

Joe, who had been told about the foal when Liz went to fetch the horse-box, had a loose-box waiting, thick with clean straw. Candy followed Lew inside without a murmur, and the foal staggered after her. Liz removed the pony's halter, put hay in the rack, and closed the half-door. The pony began to feed, and within seconds the foal had found his own nourishment and was suckling. The mare turned her head to watch him, almost as if she were surprised, and then dipped to her own meal.

'It's nice to have a foal on the place,' Liz said. She was unable to withstand the charm of tiny creatures; of calves, chasing through the meadows, of chicks, scrabbling in the dust; of lambs in the next door farm fields, crazy with pure joy of living. Even now, in her own farmyard there were pheasant chicks and turkey chicks and ducklings and goslings, as well as the litter of pups, and soon Midge would have more kittens.

'I'd like a donkey foal,' she added, and then went on to Joe's apparently unresponsive back. 'Nat suggested we bought in horses and I gave riding lessons again.'

Joe, who had been counting sacks of hen-feed beside the well, which, with its tiled roof and nursery rhyme wall, was more ornament than use, turned to face her.

'That's a damned good idea,' he said heartily. Proper

87

down in the dumps Liz was sometimes. Do her the world of good to have an interest of her own.

'You don't mind? It will be a lot more work.'

'Might find someone ready to help,' Joe was easy in his mind about that. Half the kids in the village would come and muck out for the hell of it, if he knew kids. Only got to offer them the chance of a free ride now and then and they'd work as hard as a grown man. Wasn't as if it was tricky work. And Lew would groom them, and old Nat would come and do that too, crazy about horses was old Nat. Thought the petrol engine should never have been invented.

'We'll go to the next Beast Sale and see what we can pick up,' he promised. 'And look out for adverts. And I'll tell the chaps in the Wheatsheaf to keep their ears open. Want to come down yourself tonight?'

Liz shook her head. She had better go through the papers on the desk and see there was nothing else she had overlooked. She had long ago renewed the insurance for the bull but she still felt guilty.

Casey, who was taking brief exercise in the farm yard, caught a mouse by the stack at the edge of the yard, teased Rip, the older of the two shelties, and went back to curl close to his huge companion, and dream of catching rats as large as rabbits, bringing them home proudly for all the world to see. He lay in a patch of sunlight that glinted on his shining fur and warmed him comfortably. His intermittent purr told everyone how grand life felt, and how good was his share of it.

He opened one eye and saw Liz.

He opened both eyes, washed his front paw, gave the bull's woolly hide a quick affectionate lick, stretched luxuriously, and leaped lightly to the top of the half-door. Sultan rubbed his head against the cat. Casey responded by leaning against the bull and scratching his own furry poll on the black tipped yellow horn that angled for a short distance from the beast's skull. Yawning, he jumped down and sauntered round the yard.

The foal was curious. He had fed, and slept and fed again. He had found out how to walk. He would soon be ready to be exercised in the paddock, and he could now explore the new strange place in which he found himself. He rubbed his small inquisitive nose against the white-washed bricks, sniffed the hay in his mother's hayrack, brushed against the wooden half-door over which he could see the vast arch of the murking sky, the red globe of the sun, louring over the house, the moving leaves that shirred and rustled and sissled against the tree trunk. The noise both puzzled and alarmed him, so that he whickered to his mother.

Casey heard the sound.

He paused, astonished, one paw lifted and curled. He turned his head, and saw the half-door open at the top. Heard the questioning whinny from the foal again, and sped, light-footed, over the cobbles, landing on the half-door, where he saw both Candy and the foal.

He was used to horses. Starlight, after that first crazy occasion, accepted him though he would not allow the cat to jump on to his back. Casey kept his distance, but he chased mice under the manger and often explored the loose straw in the hope of a trophy. He jumped to the ground, intent on making friends with the foal.

Everything was new to the tiny creature. The field in which he had been born, vast and green and frightening; the place in which he now found himself, enclosed by four rough walls with the wide sky beyond him, and the unknown shifting trees. Even his mother's comforting bulk was not yet familiar, although he knew that it was she who offered protection and food. He learned fast.

He saw the cat. A living moving animal, much smaller than he. He moved towards it. Candy, hearing him move, rustling the straw, turned her head and saw Casey.

Her instinct took over at once. She was all mother, fighting for her son, a jungle beast, protecting her young. There was no room in her mind for question, no pause before she acted. Her hind hoof shot out. She caught Casey with all her force, her hoof driving into his chest, lifting him high in the air. Liz saw him sail over the half-door, out into the yard, and saw him, unable to regain either breath or balance, fall heavily on to one hind leg, and roll sideways, with a wail that sickened her.

She ran to him.

He tried to move, to lick her hand, tried to show her that he was still alive, that he appreciated her solicitude. She lifted him gently and his muted purr rumbled for a second, stopped, and rumbled again, but as she moved him, the throb ceased, his eyes stared at her, blank with shock, with disbelief, with pain, and he squalled his agony.

His left hind leg hung useless, apparently disconnected from his body. Two deep wounds welled black blood that dripped on to Liz's dress, in a slow treacly ooze.

'Oh Casey!' Liz said.

She walked towards the house and Casey cuddled against her. He trusted her perfectly, sure she could make him whole again, that in her strong hands his leg would soon be put right. He lay quietly on her lap as she reached for the telephone and dialled Ken Lewis's number.

He would come at once.

Relieved, she reached for a box of tissues, to mop the welling blood. She put Casey in the box that belonged to Bennie, and stroked him gently. His eyes, watching her move away again, were bereft.

She sat down in the armchair. The cat was better lying in his box. She was dog-tired, having had little sleep the night before. Her eyes closed.

She woke to feel Casey's claws dragging at her skirt. She stared down at him. He had left his box and dragged himself across the floor. The blood trail showed the path he had taken. He wanted Liz. He wanted the comfort of her lap, the protection of her arms, the warmth of her body. He wanted the safe feeling that always filled him with bliss when Liz or Joe held him firmly in their strong hands.

Liz lifted him, hating the sight of the dangling leg that seemed not to belong to him at all. She was afraid to touch it, so she let the little beast settle himself, which he did with great difficulty, unable to understand why he had, so suddenly, no command over this part of his body, and was unable to walk or run or jump, his quick-silver movements completely destroyed in one second.

He purred as Liz stroked him, and then he closed his eyes, and the room was filled with harsh breathing. Dismayed, Liz put her hand to his chest and parted the fur, finding the skin scored and broken, and the rib cage also damaged. She looked down at the cat. She was fond of the absurd little beast. He had endearing ways, always coming to her for food, asking with his harsh cry, rubbing his head against her shoe, against the table leg, against his plate, against the refrigerator door in an unvarying ritual that never altered. When the meal was ready for him, he reached up, sitting like a begging dog, his paw urgent, clawing above his head at the plate until he had brought it down to floor level, and could sample the food, and then, if he were satisfied, lower himself slowly to a crouch, his tail moving slightly as he fed, oblivious to everything but the present moment of utter well-being.

When Lew put his head round the kitchen door to ask if he could do anything more before milking time, she called him. He came, and stood, white faced and shocked, looking down at Casey.

'Poor lil owd cat,' he said, his voice caressing, and Casey opened one eye and mewed, glad to be noticed, but too hurt to purr again. His world was suddenly encompassed by pain undreamed of, and he shuddered as he tried to move and settle again in a more comfortable position.

'Bring me some warm milk and put a spot of brandy in it,' Liz said and Lew went quickly to the cupboard.

'Poor lil owd devil,' he said again, his face contorted with concern. He brought the saucer, but Casey turned his head away.

'Poor lil beast,' said Lew.

He dipped his fingers in the milk and wetted the cat's mouth. Casey licked his lips, disliking the taste of brandy.

'Her won't die, missus?' Lew asked anxiously.

Liz could not answer. She had been wondering that herself. She stroked the cat's soft fur, and watched the dragging clock and wished that Ken would come.

Casey was so limp that she was afraid to touch him again, or lift him. If only he had not gone to look at Candy. If only she had shut the stable door completely. She might have known, had she thought, for Casey was curious and most mares would protect their young.

The room was silent except for the stir of a leaf beyond the window and the soft breath that grew fainter and fainter in the little cat's throat.

CHAPTER EIGHT

'MRS. WAYMAN?'

Liz jumped. She had not heard the knock at the door. Her attention had been concentrated on the cat, on the faint shuddering breaths that moved his small body, on the dark treacly blood that oozed continuously and unnervingly from the two deep wounds, on the faint flicker of life that seemed to be vanishing beneath her fingers, slipping away from her as the blood slipped away from the bruised flesh. Not even the soft pressure of her hands could produce a purr.

The man who stood at the door was a stranger, that she could see, even in the half light that shadowed him. He was big and burly, and, as she turned startled eyes towards him, he moved forward into the room.

'I'm sorry,' he said helplessly, looking down at her and at the cat. 'They told me to come here when I phoned Mr. Lewis.'

He came from the shadow into the light, a big man with thick curly grizzled hair, with a strong jaw and a gentle mouth, with brown eyes that reflected her own helplessness, and for the first time Liz noticed that he held a whippet in his arms.

'She's been whelping since midnight,' he said heavily.

93

'I tried to get the Vet, but kept missing him. He's run off his feet, I should think.'

'Sit down,' Liz said. She looked at the cat uncertainly. 'Would you like a drink? Some tea?'

'I'll brew tea, Mis' Liz,' Lew had taken refuge on the wide chintz-covered window seat, unable to bear watching Casey suffer, yet unable to go out and resume his own chores. He would be glad to have something to do. 'Be glad to.'

He busied himself with kettle and cups, and Liz sat silent, not knowing what to say, wishing the Vet would hurry, and suddenly painfully aware that to Casey's sobbing breath was added the forlorn whimpers of the little bitch, as she writhed on her master's knee.

'Casey got kicked by a pony,' she said, feeling utterly futile, yet aware that the situation would be eased by conversation.

'Poor little devil. He looks in a bad way.' The visitor was glad to talk, suddenly wanting to share himself and this moment, knowing that both of them suffered for their animals. 'I'm Michael Flynn, from the Cottage.'

The Cottage was half-way through the village, an old thatched stone building which belonged to the Wheatsheaf. She knew that it had recently been let.

'You only moved in last week.' It was better to go on talking, to pretend the animals were not there, to forget for an instant the pain that mocked both helpless owners, to the frantic panting whines of the little bitch, the soft ever-lessening sounds of Casey's breathing.

He nodded, a big bulky man, with an odd air of reassurance about him, although he was as worried as she.

'Funny, coming to a village,' he said reflectively, watching a mote of sunlight dazzle on the stirrup of the hunter's saddle. 'Always lived in a city. It's quiet, here.

And peaceful. In spite of all the animal noises. Always wanted to retire into the country . . . and yet, somehow, I miss the city. Miss my job.'

'You'll find it strange,' Liz said. 'I don't suppose you're used to animals, coming from a built-up place.'

She was about to say more, but Michael Flynn's face creased in sudden genuine amusement.

'Not cattle,' he said. 'But I'm used to horses. I was a mounted policeman.'

Liz's mouth curved in a rueful half-grin.

'You must indeed be used to horses,' she said. 'You'll miss them.'

'Horribly. I wanted to ask you if I could help out sometimes with your hunter – don't want paying – just to be with a horse again. Heard about him at the Wheatsheaf. Only . . . I didn't think we'd meet like this.' He eased the bitch into a more comfortable position on his lap. She was a delicate creature, all bone and muscle and elegance, which showed still in spite of the pups within her. Her small sharp-muzzled head lifted to look at him, her glowing brown eyes, darkened with pain, stared up at him, aware that he wanted to help, and grateful for the comfort of his hands on her tortured body. Her sleek fur was creamy fawn, thistledown soft. Slender ears moved as she moved her head, and then, whimpering again, she turned herself round, and flopped across his knees, giving his sunburnt hand a swift grateful lick.

'She's exhausted.' He looked down at her, wishing he knew what to do. He was sure the first pup was crosswise, but he dared not find out, dared not touch her lest he injure her. They had warned him at the kennels that she was very small and that whippets found birth difficult. He wished he had not tried to breed from her. This was too cruel.

He took the tea that Lew had brewed. It was dark, with floating tea leaves and with skin from the boiled milk from the morning coffee, but it was hot and distracting. He smoothed the bitch's coat and looked across at Liz. The paper tissues in her hand were soaked with blood, and her blue dress was dark and stained. If only the Vet would come. If only he could put back the clock – he looked down at the bitch. Never again.

'It's funny,' he said, speaking his thoughts aloud, musing suddenly over the past few months. 'You do a job for the better part of your life, day in, day out, just a few days a year off for a holiday . . . and then, quite suddenly, it stops. Everything stops. You go down to the stables, and you're a stranger. There isn't a horse that's yours. The men don't quite know what to say to you, you're not part of the routine, you're the old fellow come back on a visit, and you feel in the way. I wanted to go back, to see them all, after six months off the job . . . and there were new faces there, men I'd never seen before who didn't know me, and two new horses. And my old lass was gone. I knew that, of course, but it seemed all wrong, not to find her in her stall, but to find a big grey there instead who flattened his ears and pawed the ground when he saw me. That's why we moved. Soul destroying – retirement in a city.'

'What happened to your mare?' Liz asked. The tea was terrible, but Lew had meant well, and she smiled at him. He did not see her, his eyes only had room for the little cat. If lil owd Casey died what'd come of owd bull? Pine away and fret, not a doubt. Lew tried to drink his own tea, but his worries were so big that he could not swallow and left most of it untouched.

'She died,' Michael Flynn said. 'It was queer, that. Just a few days before I left. I was glad, in a way. She was due to retire too and that means a bullet for a police horse. Can't put her out to graze, you see, she's been a pampered darling all her life, manger-fed three times a day, and groomed and kept in a warm stable. Put her in a field to graze and she'd get an aching neck and probably die of cold. It's hard, but you've no choice.'

'I can see that,' Liz said. A lot of things were hard, but there was never any choice. You learned to endure them. Like the bull. She wanted distraction from that thought too.

'She was a beauty,' Michael Flynn said, seeing too vividly into the past. Seeing the warm friendly stables where the horses stood in rows, each under his own name. Sirius, Saturn, Pluto, Neptune, Orion, a starry galaxy with his own dark bay Thetis always waiting for him, turning her head, calling eagerly as soon as she heard her master's footstep. Thetis, who had been so easy to train, so unafraid of noise, of crowds, of fireworks and shouting, so well drilled that she knew, almost without a signal, when to back and when to half-pass, when to lean against an unruly crowd member, when to stand rock-like, unmoving, not flinching even if a small child crawled between her hooves and used her legs to pull himself erect, never treading on a fallen man, never turning a hair in hottest sunshine or in a crackling thunderstorm.

There had been good days, wonderful days, in the past, he thought, staring down at the whippet bitch, but, for the moment, not seeing her. The days of the big shows, when each man dressed in his ceremonial uniform, gleaming saddles and bridles, glittering breast chains, cavalry boots, the dashing white plumed helmets, the lances with their coloured standards and the sudden joyous surge as each man in turn galloped down the track to spear a piece of card from the ground, swinging from the saddle and back in one swift movement, holding the trophy aloft. The movements of the figure-of-eight, crossing, criss-crossing, each perfect in his pattern as the horses passed and re-passed in low movement, and the crowd watched, enthralled.

'She was a great mare, Thetis,' Michael Flynn said, but he wasn't talking to Liz, he was thinking aloud, remembering. 'Gentle as a lamb. And affectionate. Always used to lick me with her great floppy tongue when I came on duty, and when I fed her. Never nipped or kicked or bit. Stood like an idol when we clipped her. Not like some of them. Old Jupiter now, he was good as gold except when we used the clippers on him and then he went mad. Took six men and six ropes to hold him, and then took about six hours' work to get him ready. Loathed every second of it. And Pluto, grooming tickled him, and he'd rub and wriggle against the side of his stall and then nibble the top, nearly daft with the movement of the brush. Good as gold otherwise, but it seemed to affect him the way tickling does some people. Only horses can't laugh.'

'Starlight does that, my husband's hunter,' Liz said, wondering why when you were waiting for a particular car there suddenly seemed to be dozens roaring up the lane, and driving past again. Normally, she'd have sworn, there were hardly any. What on earth had happened to Ken?

'Had a pal, had Thetis.' Michael Flynn was using his voice as an anodyne now, talking for the sake of it, suddenly aware that the little bitch was soothed by the sound of the words, and that Liz was almost mesmerized, her strained expression easing. 'A little black cat. A little battered tom cat, a real warrior, with one torn ear, and one blind eye, and a lame leg and the scars of as many

98

battles on him as there are flowers in your garden. Used to come in every night, summer and winter, and sleep on the mare's neck. Thetis got to looking for him, and then she couldn't rest until the cat came. Terrific bond between those two. But one day Tommy didn't turn up. We found him next morning lying in the gutter. A car had killed him. Thetis fretted for him. Waited each night, her eyes on the doorway. Called sometimes, the night watchman said, as if she was calling the little cat home. But Tommy never came, and Thetis wouldn't eat properly, wouldn't do anything with any heart in her. She'd come out with me, greet me as she always did, but somehow all the life seemed to have gone from her. No lift when she trotted. Not much response when I called her, not even if I brought carrots for her. And then, one morning, I turned up for work and found the night man with her, and her dead in her stall. Heart attack, the Vet said. It wasn't a heart attack. It was a broken heart. Sounds daft, but that's what it was.'

The silence after the words was unendurable. There was a tap dripping in the kitchen sink, and the dreadful sound of the busy clock flying through the minutes, tick, tick, tick, insistently, yet time stood still in spite of it, the hands refusing to follow the hurrying wheels. Casey sighed deeply, and then moved himself uneasily. He lifted hazed green eyes and stared at Liz as if he were gazing into her soul, begging her to help him. His body shook, and she realized suddenly that he was shivering. She hadn't even thought of shock.

'Get me a rug, quickly, Lew,' she said. 'Casey's cold.'

'Shock.' Michael Flynn wished he had thought of it before. He should have realized. But all his mind had been on his own troubles, and he stroked Shanie and wished the Vet would hurry. 'A hot water bottle would

99

help. And some warm milk with just a few drops of brandy.'

'I don't think he'll drink,' Liz said.

'A medicine dropper. You can put it down his throat then. Where in Heaven's name is that Vet?'

Lew might be slow, but he needed no second telling. He brought the rug and found the hot water bottle that was kept for ailing beasts. There were often a couple of chicks or a lamb from the next farm to nurse. Liz helped out whenever she was wanted. She enjoyed looking after animals. They were so helpless and showed so much gratitude.

Joe, coming into the room, having walked across the far field to look at the cows, was full of himself and his success at the Sale. He was longing to tell Liz about the mare he had bought for her, and the two ponies that a farmer on the other side of the county had promised for her new venture. He stopped and stared in astonishment before he flung his jacket down on the window seat.

'What goes on?' he asked.

'Casey's got kicked by Candy ... his leg's broken, and he's very bad ... and Mr. Flynn's bitch is in trouble. She's been whelping since midnight.'

Joe bent over the cat, and then took the medicine dropper from Lew who had filled it with warm milk to which he added a few drops of brandy. Casey did not resist at all when his head was lifted and his mouth was opened. Joe stroked his throat and the warm liquid went down smoothly and the small head drooped again.

'I wish Ken would come,' Liz said. Waiting was hell, waiting was worse than anything in the world, whatever it was you waited for ... and this was worst of all.

Joe was bending over the little bitch. He was used to

birth and could deliver an awkward calf as swiftly and easily as the Vet, knowing how to fix the ropes and ease curled legs that prevented birth. His exploring hands felt the pup's body.

'Cross-wise. Ken'll have to do a Caesarian,' he said.

'Thought so.' Michael Flynn sighed. He was worn out with lack of sleep and with waiting. If only a man wasn't so damned helpless ... if only ... if ifs and ans were pots and pans, his mind thought rebelliously recalling an old childhood rhyme. Idiotic the way one's thoughts played up and took over.

The sound of the engine in the yard brought Lew from the scullery and Joe to the door. Ken jumped out, and pushed back the hair from his eyes with a quick irritable gesture.

'What's up?' he asked. 'Cat worse?'

'Her's goin' to die,' Lew said forlornly, suddenly voicing his own private fear. Ken looked at him, and then swallowed the impatient words that had come to mind. He'd have to get a partner. Out all night on a case of suspected anthrax, and the case confirmed at that, so that he had to kill the animal and see it burnt and his own private terror didn't help. Scared stiff of anthrax. Beastly thing, one of the few animal diseases a man could catch, and a killer at that. Why in hell had he become a Vet and not a stockbroker?

But when he went into the room and saw the cat and saw the bitch he knew the answer. His skill was needed, and he shed irritation and tiredness like a snake sloughing its skin.

He went to the bitch and looked at her.

'I'll have to operate and quick,' he said. 'Can I do it here, Joe?'

'I'll get the foaling room ready,' Joe said. He used it

for the cattle. There was a marble topped table there that could easily be scrubbed, the light was good, and there was a sterilizer. He was used to immunizing his own cattle, or to giving a cow with milk fever a dose of calcium boroglucinate, or having to give antibiotics when necessary. Ken diagnosed and left him to carry out the treatment. It saved time for both of them. And there were always abscesses to be lanced, and other surgical jobs that needed doing. A farmer needed to know a good deal about veterinary work if he wasn't to spend a fortune on vet bills.

'She'll do for a few minutes more, poor beast,' Ken said. He stroked the whippet's soft head and she looked up at him, trusting him. It never failed to astonish him, the way animals seemed to know that he was there to help. There was a little tiger tabby cat next door but two to him that had been brought to him with an abscess, and now whenever Tigger got into the wars, he came visiting on his own, miaowing to be let in, taking his injuries to Ken to look at, quite certain that this was the correct thing to do. Ken could never bring himself to send in a bill for his services when the cat had come by himself.

He bent over Casey.

'Shock, mostly,' he said at last. He filled the syringe with penicillin, and the cat did not open even one eye as the needle sank into his shoulder. 'Let him rest and I'll X-ray that leg in the morning.' Ken was proud of his new X-ray equipment and it saved endless time. Could diagnose at once without needing to send the animal elsewhere. 'Casey will be all right, I'm pretty sure. He's tough. Just keep him quiet tonight and don't let him move.'

'Those two holes in his thigh?' Liz wished the bleeding would stop.

'Splintered bone,' Ken said shortly. 'There's no need to worry, Liz. Honestly. Put him in a box and keep him warm. He'll be much better by morning. The injection will help. It's mainly shock that's the trouble.'

Liz put the cat in the box and went out to help Lew with the afternoon milking. Cherry was irritable, unusually so. They had been hoping that she was in-calf, but there was no sign of it. Have to put her to the bull again. She stamped when they went to put her in the milking parlour, and most unusually, angled a horn at Lew, and then butted him savagely so that he slipped, banging his elbow on the partition between the cows.

He stood up, uncomplaining, and bent to look at her. Then he whistled.

'Had visitors, Mis' Liz,' he said. 'Her's got a fishing 'ook stook in leg.'

'Good job Ken's here,' Liz said, inspecting Cherry's leg. The length of nylon trace had caught above the knee, and twisted down round her hock, and the hook itself, a sizeable thing used for coarse fishing, had penetrated the flesh just beneath it. Someone had been poaching in the little river that fed the cattle pond, a favourite wading place of Cherry's.

Michael Flynn stood at the door watching them. He felt useless, and wished he had gone with Joe and the Vet to operate on the bitch. He wondered about anaesthetics, wondered about the difficulty of surgery outside, wondered if the puppies would be alive after so long and so much straining, wondered if the bitch would survive. She had been so exhausted, poor brute. He had grown fond of her in the ten months that she had been his. She had been found emaciated by an RSPCA Inspector, and when no one claimed her, he had bought her for twenty-five shillings from the dog pound. He hated the pound. Stray dogs howled continuously, wanting their owners, lonely, bewildered, and miserable.

'Do a few owners good to be locked up here,' the sergeant in charge of the police dogs had said in fury one day, when a small spaniel bitch had howled so heart-rendingly that she had upset all the police dogs and turned the station into temporary bedlam.

Mike could not rest. The cattle were milling in the yard, and he pushed his way through them, looking in briefly at the bull, who was irritated by flies that pestered him, circling his ears and settling in the wet tracks beneath his eyes. He tossed his head, scraped his horn noisily on the wall, and snorted, pawing the ground.

'Poor old fellow,' Mike Flynn said.

He left the brooding beast, and turned to the stable, knowing that here he could lose his worries temporarily. It had been a long time since he had handled a horse. He went to the half-door. They had told him about Starlight, down at the Wheatsheaf, and he had seen Joe taking the hunter for rare exercise, and admired the sweep of him, the proud lift of his arched neck, the flowing movement when he cantered, the lift of mane and tail. He had watched at a distance, almost sick with envy and with the memory of his bay Thetis, his beauty, his for twenty long years, day after day, tending and grooming, feeding and training, riding every day on duty and at the big ceremonies. The horse was part of him, although it did not belong to him, it was his for duration of his time in the Force, and as much his as if he had owned it.

He called to Starlight, an odd sound, half-way between a snort and a whistle, and the horse, bored and lonely, responded eagerly, came at once, recognizing a man who understood him and how he felt, leaned against the caressing hand, nuzzling into it asking to be petted.

'You beauty!' Mike Flynn looked at the horse. 'You beauty.'

He was inside the stable, picking up the curry brush, remembering the rhythm of grooming a horse with military precision, a cavalry exercise that all policemen used. He whistled softly, absorbed, the brush movements long and rhythmic, and the horse revelled in them, in the feel of strong hands working him, in a grooming such as he had never known before for Joe had not time or training to treat him like this and Liz had not the strength.

The hindquarters were gleaming, polished and shining, and Mike had set to work on the massive shoulders when Joe put his head through the door, and whistled at the sight of the hunter.

'He's never looked like that in his life!' he said, looking at the sheen that was building up in the handsome coat. The mane lay silken, in a long glossy sweep, the tail was perfect, and Starlight tossed his head, as if aware of his beauty and showing off in his pride.

'He's a good horse,' Mike Flynn said, patting the animal firmly on the withers. Starlight tossed his head, turned it swiftly and rubbed it against the man in delight, revelling in attention at this unusual hour, and men about him, with time for him for a change, and not just a quick word and a swift pat and then left to himself bored and lonely in his stable.

'Joe! Where the hell's that box?' Ken yelled from the foaling room, having done his job well, and lost his temper again from sheer weariness. His head was stuffed with cotton wool, his eyes gummed open and aching, and every bone in him screamed for rest, and Joe was lingering, gossiping, with no thought for anyone else.

Joe realized his fault at once, and ran to the house,

returning a few minutes later with a wooden box lined with an old woollen jersey. Ken put the pups inside, and looked up to find Mike staring down at them.

'They're O.K.?' he asked, disbelief in his voice. Tiny little Shanie could never, in a month of rainbow days, have given birth to all these.

'They're fine. Eight of them. The first one's dead.' The minute body lay on the table, and Shanie herself, still unconscious, lay on straw in the corner. Mike walked across to look at her, noticing the still bleeding cut and the incredibly neat stitches that held the edges together. He went back to the puppies, and looked down at them, minute scraps of life, blind eyes closed, delicate claws on tiny paws that moved feebly to the accompaniment of faint whimpers.

'I'll put them by the fire,' Liz said, coming in wearily after milking, with a bruise on one arm from Cherry's horn, and a bang on her leg where Bluebell had kicked her. The cows resented any change in handling, preferred Joe to her, always, and the milk yield was down. Funny how the cows held on to their milk when a stranger handled them, even with the milking machine. She remembered a man they had had five years ago, a man called Higgins, who'd been a marvel with the cattle, got twice the yield from all of them. Unfortunately he was never sober and his unpredictable habits made it impossible to keep him. She lifted the box, marvelling at the little writhing bodies. It always amazed her that anything so small could be so fiercely alive.

Casey was asleep, his head tucked under his front paws, his body half sprawled, the injured leg stretched out uselessly behind him. The slow blood-ooze had almost stopped. She put a hand to the cat, and he flicked his ears and shook his head and gave a quiet breathy purr, and then curled back to sleep, lulled by the injection that Ken had given him.

The kettle was boiling. Liz made more tea, and poured mugs for the men. She took a drink to Lew, who was hosing down the slimy yard, and he nodded to her.

'Lil owd dog's awake,' he said. 'Her's whimpering.'

Ken went back to look at the bitch. She was woozy from the anaesthetic, trying to stand, but reeling across the floor, shaking her head, whimpering and bewildered. He lifted her and took her into the kitchen, where Mike waited.

'Good lass,' he said, and the bitch held out her paws to him, flailing them urgently, so that he took her and she settled at once in his arms, utterly content, her tail wagging feebly to show her pleasure, her tongue warm on his chin.

'Let her rest and then show her the pups,' Ken said. He drained his mug and went out again to the far part of the stables, where Cherry had been put to wait until he could remove the hook. It had gone deep, and he muttered furiously under his breath as he worked, damning all fishermen and all trippers who came and left their rubbish where it could do harm and make more work for him.

'You're the fifth this week,' he told Cherry, as she swished her tail across his mouth and nosed him, easing her leg away from him, unwisely shifting to balance most of her weight on his foot. 'Off and be damned to you, idiot cow. Five bloody beasts this week; a fish hook,' he ripped it out, dabbed at the bleeding flesh, and patted the cow on the head, 'and a bloody big one, you poor brute, going to catch whales, that feller, and two legs cut to the bone on two dogs from broken glass, and a cat run over by a maniac in the lane, speeding round a blind corner at a million miles an hour; and a pig with a polythene bag in his guts; and a sheep with flaming food poisoning, God knows what it ate. Damn all townsfolk.' He patted Cherry again. She could move her leg, and bend it, although the cut was sore, and she was feeling better-tempered. She mooed at him, an asinine reply that always made Lew and Joe laugh and made Ken grin. 'You're a daft old beast.'

He went back to the kitchen and re-filled his mug, and stood glowering into the fire, too tired to answer when Liz spoke to him. Recognizing the symptoms she left him alone.

He would have to go home. With a bit of luck, he might manage to sleep for a couple of hours before evening surgery. His mother would have hot soup waiting for him. She had learned long ago that it was a waste of time to get a meal ready for him. Soup was always reviving and while he drank it she could cook him a steak or an omelet. It would be nice to sit down to a meal one day, he thought, his mind flicking impotently from one idea to another. Soup. A chicken and stuffing and onion sauce and roast potatoes and peas, and a decent pudding. Last time his mother had made a meal like that the police had come for him. Taken him along the motorway where some blind young fool in a fast car had skidded into a totter and his pony. Ken swallowed. It had been his nightmare for too long, the pony lying on the verge with its body twisted and torn wide open, and the crumpled car, and the blood in the road, and the old man in his ragged overcoat sitting on the grass with the dying beast's head in his lap and the tears pouring down his dirty cheeks, saying over and over, 'I'd like to kill him, I'd like to kill him,' oblivious of the fact that the police sergeant had told him that the driver too was dead. He had administered the final coup de grace. The pony's screams had stopped and his eyes had glazed and Ken had left the scene behind him, and driven home through the blue day and seen the daffodils duck their heads under the wind. And been greeted by his own dog, a magnificent golden retriever, running to jump at him. He had gone indoors, to find that his mother had saved his food for him, and the food choked him so that he took the dog and went walking in the wild wind, across the hills and through the budding new growth of the season's heather, with hate in him for the machines that could cause so much destruction and leave a horse to scream its last breath away and an old man to sit and sorrow in the midday sun.

It came back to him, whenever he was tired, and today he was dog-tired. He wanted to go and see Sue, and take her dancing, and forget his job for a few hours, savouring the scent of her hair, and the feel of her in his arms. There was no time for courtship. No time for love, no time for leisure.

'You must get a partner, Ken,' Joe said, looking anxiously at the Vet. Ken's skin was stretched taut across his face, his mouth was tight, his eyes stared from a mask of exhaustion.

'I've advertised. Not many men want to cope with large animals. Everyone seems to prefer a town practice. Less driving around and more money.'

Ken lifted the whippet gently. She relaxed in his hands, and he laid her on the table and pressed his fingers gently round the wound. She gave no sign of pain, other than a small whimper. He nodded, satisfied, and then lifted her to the floor and put her beside the box, where the pups were moving in much more lively fashion, sprawling across each other, small stump tails weaving gently, small paws scrabbling, small mouths lifting and seeking, small voices whimpering.

Shanie took one look at the pups and wailed, her muzzle lifted to the rafters. She backed away, growling at the pups, and fled beneath the dresser, only her black nose and brown desperate eyes showing.

'What in the world . . . ?' Mike said in astonishment.

'She thinks she's done wrong,' Ken said, his voice amused. He bent to the whippet. 'Here girl. Good girl. Clever girl.'

'Good Shanie. Here lass, good Shanie.' Mike joined him, and Liz smiled quietly to herself at the sight of the two huge men down on their knees, peering under the dresser, uttering blandishments to the dog.

Shanie was forlorn. She had spent the night in agony, twisted with such pain as she had never known in her life. She had woken with an odd taste in her mouth and a weird feeling in her legs, which refused to obey her. She had a sore tummy that hurt when she moved, and now they showed her a box full of incredible objects, obviously alive, but nothing like any animal that she had ever seen, and smelling, moreover, of strange human hands. She was not going to venture back to that if she could help it.

Ken put his hand under the dresser. Shanie, bewildered, still half drugged by the anaesthetic, and tested beyond endurance, sank her fangs deep into the skin. Ken swore. The bitch had bitten right to the bone.

'I'm taking you to the doctor with that,' Joe said firmly, looking at the hand. 'Could go septic. You need an injection.'

'Rubbish.' Ken was irritable, and furious because he had not used his imagination. He should have known that she would react like that in fright. That's what came of being tired.

'You can do as you're told,' Liz said, smiling to ease the curtness of her words. 'Better be safe than sorry.'

Mike had coaxed Shanie to him. She was trembling, aware that she had added crime to the odd circumstances in which she found herself.

'Sit in the big chair and let her have one of the pups with her,' Liz said. 'It's just shock, and she's never seen puppies before. She'll get over it.'

Mike dropped gratefully into the vast wicker chair that creaked under his weight. Liz lifted the biggest pup, and he took it in his hand, where it nestled comfortably, warm, secure, and almost completely hidden. He held the pup to the bitch. She turned her head away, gazed up at him pleadingly and whimpered again.

The pup stretched and put out a pink tongue that was no bigger than a finger nail. It squeaked. Shanie's ears moved, but she did not look at it. Her nose began to wrinkle as she sniffed. There was a faint scent about the creature ... a teasingly reminiscent scent, a fractionally pleasurable scent. ... She turned her head and sniffed again and her small son moved himself so that his body was against hers, and his mouth began seeking, seeking, turning blindly, hunting for milk.

He began to suck. Shanie turned her head, startled. She bent and smelt the pup. Her instinct, dormant no longer, flared to life, and her tongue began its task of cleaning and grooming, lick, lick, licking away until the down was wet.

'Put her in the box,' Ken said.

Mike moved the pups and put the whippet with them. She began to sniff at them, and then stretched herself out, and the eight thrusting babies climbed against her, pushing and scratching with transparent claws.

Ken drove away to visit the doctor and to try and find

time for sleep, and Joe and Liz made more tea and helped Mike celebrate.

But every third minute Liz turned her head to look at Casey, curled, fast asleep, the broken leg angled along his black body, and it was all she could do to stop herself from lifting him to make sure that he was still breathing.

CHAPTER NINE

Casey woke, to find that the world had darkened without his knowledge. Day had vanished, and night slipped in, with a moon that hung low and bland and shone through the window, casting flecked shadows on the stone floor. Outside, in the shady fields, the cows called to one another, a calf lowed for its mother, a sheep bleated, far away. Starlight whinnied to an imaginary mare, or perhaps to Candy, herself occupied with her small long-legged son, and an owl wailed its hunger to the pinpoint stars.

Casey lay and considered, until the desolate call of the lonely bull jogged him to startled consciousness, so that he was unaware of a faint background hunger, of a raging thirst, of a reluctance to move, and fully aware that now he should be out in the stall with the bull, not lying in the kitchen, alone in the dark.

He stood. The useless leg was heavy and dangled on the floor behind him. He turned to examine it, and then, as Sultan lowed again, he began to move, hobbling on three legs, shuffling over the floor. It took ten minutes to shift his body as many feet, but Casey was persistent.

Liz woke to hear the odd noise below her. Frowning, she pulled on jersey and slacks. Few emergencies on a farm could be dealt with in a dressing gown.

Casey was half-way across the floor, moonlight shining on him as he shifted himself awkwardly, shuffle, slide and stop . . . shuffle, slide and stop. He heard Liz coming, and flopped down and wailed, a small, almost unrecognizable, peevish sound. Joe, waking to find Liz gone, heard the noise and came to the top of the stairs to investigate. He found Liz bending over the cat. The two deep holes were bleeding again, and the end of a splintered bone was visible. Liz swallowed.

'He shouldn't be moving at all,' she said desperately. 'I wish I could tie that leg up.'

'He'd only spend his time tugging at the bandages,' Joe said, long experience of many cats behind him. None of them had ever tolerated a bandage or dressing of any kind, and one small tabby, his leg broken when he was run over by a bicycle, had spent a night chewing off the plaster of Paris that the Vet put on to hold the bones together, and Joe had found him in the morning surrounded by chewed plaster, the leg once more at an angle, but the cat purring and apparently well content. The second time he had stayed at the Vet's house, in a small cage, with a collar round his neck to keep him from trying the same trick again.

The bull lowed, all desolation in the sound. Casey's ears pricked, he lifted his head, animation came back into his eyes, and he yowled, a louder sound this time.

'Dammit, he wants to get to the bull,' Joe said, looking at the small animal, now on three legs once more, trailing himself determinedly towards the door.

'What can we do with him?' Liz asked. She pushed her hair out of her eyes and yawned. The clock in the big drawing-room tinkled the chimes, and struck one.

Joe went into the kitchen and came back with a small box with high sides. He padded it with newspaper, and started to put Casey inside. Casey, frustrated, in pain, bewildered by his own inability to run and jump as he always did, arched his back in sudden temper, spat, and struck out with his forepaw, falling sideways in the process. He stared up at Joe with desperately unhappy eyes. He had never attempted to scratch any human creature before.

'Never mind, feller.' Joe's voice was soothing. 'Come on, then, we'll see to you.'

He lifted the cat into the box. This time Casey did not protest. It was too much effort to struggle, or to move, with pain raging in his hind leg, and a throbbing in his paw, and his whole body aching from the bruising he had received when he fell. He wailed again, a cry of frustration that died away, and left him staring, wide-eyed, as Joe opened the door into the yard and carried him outside.

Moonlight trellised the cobbles. A faint stamping came from Starlight's stall, and a soft snort from Candy, who woke up, her ears eager, as she listened to the footfall in the yard. She nuzzled her foal protectively. The dreaming cattle came to the field gate, curious. Cherry watched as Joe unfastened the door of the bull-pen.

Sultan turned his head, caught the scent of the cat, and lowed loudly, welcoming the small animal. Casey's ears pricked forward, and he yowled his reply. Joe put the box down, and at once the bull nosed it, catching the sudden rank smell of blood. His tongue licked out, caressing the fur, cleaning the injury. He settled in the straw. Joe left them, and the bull lay with his head beside Casey's box. Casey stretched out his forepaw and found comfort, leaning hot pads against the huge beast's soft cheek.

Sun-up found Lew wakeful and desperately worried.

Even in his sleep he had seen Casey's small body walking uneasily, the leg dangling. If lil owd cat died, what of owd bull? And what of owd bull last night, without lil cat? Lew tossed and turned, and as the first blackbird called a carillon to the sun, he dressed himself, and went out into the dew wet day, as peal upon peal resounded, rising to the full chorus of small throats rejoicing in waking again to live yet another day in a world that offered them an ultimate peak of living, a delight of sunshine and abundant food, and the wild pleasure of flight through the warming air, of riding the wind and flashing towards the sun. Lew watched a lark spiral high into the blue, heard him bell his praise as he flighted; heard a thrush rouse and rhapsodize the heavens, saw a blackbird preen and then call and call again, his small throat trembling, his head high, his pleasure extreme and vocal.

Lew took the crust of bread he had purloined on his way from the kitchen and broke it for the birds, reserving only a corner for himself. Mis' Liz always gave him breakfast. Fear for Casey and for the bull haunted him, and he broke into a run, arriving at the farm breathless, long before Joe was even thinking of milking. He trod quietly, not wishing to wake his employers.

Starlight heard him, recognized his footsteps, and called his greeting, so that Lew, to quieten the stallion, opened the half-door, and rubbed noses with the horse, feeling, as always, the utter ecstasy of fondling the soft warm pelt, of the velvet lips that nuzzled against his hands, of the wise glow of the brilliant eyes that gazed reflectively at him.

He tedded hay into the manger, and left the horse feeding. All was quiet in the bull-pen, but he glanced inside, and then looked down, startled. Casey still slept inside his box, and his small paw rested, as it had done the night through, against the bull's cheek. The cat roused, and yawned, and stretched, the paw patting.

'Hey, owd Casey, then,' Lew said, vast relief flooding him. He went into the pen. Sultan stirred but did not move. He watched as the boy bent over the box. Casey lifted his head and licked Lew's hand, and then lapsed into a soft, breathy, almost inaudible purr.

'Her's purring,' he said to Liz, as she came round the corner of the pen. Liz looked down and saw Casey regarding her from inscrutable green eyes.

'I wonder if he'll eat,' she said. 'Bring him into the kitchen, Lew, please.' Liz was not going into the bull-pen. Even now, she felt Sultan's eyes upon her, and interpreted the look in them as baleful. Absurdly, she found herself wondering if he knew how much she hated him. Joe always said that animals were telepathic, and that horses in particular knew when a novice was on their backs, and played up accordingly. As if reading her mind, Sultan climbed clumsily to his feet, hindlegs, then forelegs, and stood looking at her, his head lowered, sweeping horns swaying as he swayed his neck. Liz backed away hurriedly.

She went to the pantry to find a tin of condensed milk, which Casey loved to steal. This time he could have it legally, and perhaps he would lap at it, even if he did not want any other food. She took his meat from the refrigerator and chopped it up, adding hot water to warm it. Lew held the plate, but the cat, after one sniff, turned his head away. Liz brought him water, and he drank greedily. She brought the condensed milk.

Casey sniffed at the saucer. Considering, he dipped his tongue. He began to lap, slowly at first, and then, as the taste pervaded his mouth, he licked greedily. Before the last drops had gone, Liz added a few drops of brandy from a medicine dropper, and the cat left the saucer clean. That, at least, was something, and she grinned up at Joe as he came yawning into the kitchen.

'Well, Lew, how about the cows?'

Lew had forgotten about milking. Guiltily, he whistled to the dogs and went hastily to the field, opening the gate to let the cattle through. They knew that it was past time, they were uncomfortable, and it was late. They shouldered past, pushing, vying with each other for first in the yard, the dogs running round them, yapping at their heels. Cherry, overeager, butted Lew impatiently and he slid to the ground, narrowly avoiding the tramping hooves as he rolled quickly away.

Like a cat himself, Liz thought, as she climbed into the Land-Rover, with Casey lying beside her in a wire cage that Ken Lewis had left for her the night before. Life was not so terrifying when the world could be seen. Liz had never met a cat that enjoyed being shut in a basket.

'It's a hell of a break,' Ken Lewis said, some time later, looking at the X-ray pictures before him. Casey, still in his wire cage, lay sleepily, apparently taking very little interest in the world. Ken bathed the two deep wounds, straightened the leg, and gave the cat an antibiotic injection. Casey was sleepy and unconcerned. He snored faintly as he breathed.

Ken's finger pointed to the picture.

'It's broken here, right where the head of the bone goes into the socket,' he said, pointing to the head of the thigh bone. 'Snapped clean off. There isn't a thing I can do.'

'You won't have to put him down,' Liz said. Not Casey, with his quicksilver jumps and his endearing ways. She looked at the small humped body, and even as she looked,

Casey flicked his ear as if he were listening to them, instantly responsive to the sound of her voice.

'No need for that. I've seen that sort of break before. It heals itself. He might be a bit slow on his feet when he recovers, and one leg will probably be shorter than the other, but he'll be mousing as good as ever in six months' time.'

'What do we do for him?' Liz asked.

'Keep him in the cage. Unless you'd rather he stayed here?' Ken was not anxious to have another patient. It was hard to get a reliable girl to look after the animals, and his mother was already overworked. She had the major responsibility, and as well as his patients there was a baby badger sow being milk-fed by bottle, after her mother had been run down on the road. One of the farm hands from the Mapley Estate had brought her in, after finding her crying beside her dead dam, trying to evoke a response from the lifeless beast. And there were two young squirrels, and the five cats that were in kennels while their owners were away. Casey would be a headache.

Leaving Casey would be too difficult, Liz decided. Somehow he would have to stay with the bull. Both animals would be happier.

'I'll take him home,' she said. She lifted the cage, prepared to take Casey out of it.

'Leave him there for a fortnight,' Ken said. 'It will give his leg a chance to start healing. The bone will knit, and by the end of that time he'll start to try his weight on it. He's better not moving about at first. Can you cope with an earth box for him?'

It was an idiotic question, and Ken realized as soon as he'd said it, and grinned. Liz was usually to be found with a pitchfork, mucking out the hunter's stall, or the cow byres where the new calves spent their first days. She often thought she was handier with a pitchfork than with a cooking pot.

Casey, taken home and left in his cage, was fretful. He wanted comfort, and daytime comfort meant Liz. Every time she passed him, he reached a paw towards her, and wailed forlornly, a miserable noise that harked back to his kitten days. At last, unable to stand the sound any longer, Liz sat in a chair and took the cat on her knee. He lay, thoughtfully staring up at her, and as her hand smoothed his coat, he began to purr softly.

He was feeling better. Not well, or whole, but better, and he had neglected his grooming. Carefully and slowly, he began to lick his forepaws, washing industriously down the length of each leg and between each pad. It was an exhausting process, and he tired quickly. He washed Liz's hand, to show that he knew she was taking care of him, and then, with a deep shuddering sigh, he curled his head under his two front paws and went to sleep, while Liz sat in the shady kitchen, watching the sun creep over the floor, hearing the little clock chime the tinkling quarters, the sleepy sound of the cattle mooing in the nearby field, the drone of a bee busy among the pinks, the soft throbbing purr of little Midge, curled on the windowsill in the sun. It was too much, and when Joe came in he found Liz asleep, with the cat curled comfortably against her, the kitchen shady, the sun gone round the corner to spill among the lengthening shadows beyond the bull-pen.

Gently, Joe ruffled his wife's hair, and went to put the kettle on for tea.

CHAPTER TEN

When bedtime came Liz put Casey's cage down by the hearth. He sat up, forlorn, staring at her. He loathed the cage, the confining wire, the indignity of the earth box put for him. He wailed.

'Now what do we do?' Liz knew from experience that the wails would continue all night. There was no creature more persistent than a Siamese, and Casey had inherited all Tartar's firmness. Casey yowled.

Joe looked at him. No use asking for silence. Who ever heard of an obedient cat? Tich, puzzled by the cage and the loud wailing, added an uncertain mournful whine to the din. The shelties, just to show companionship, barked from their kennel, and Bennie, on duty in the yard, afraid that some intruder might have crept up on him unperceived, cruised around the cobbles, alternately sniffing out strangers and growling in a deep throated continuous grumble that set the bull to lowing and the hunter to whinnying, while Candy's foal, excited by the unusual noises added his own small contribution and Candy, disturbed, added hers.

From three fields away came the yelling bray of old Jokey, Nat's jenny donkey, always willing to hold converse at any hour of the day or night and delighted by the turmoil.

'Oh, hell!' Joe said irritably. 'Casey, you're a pest.'

Casey, pleased to find that he was not to be ignored, purred companionably, and Joe switched off the light. 'Now shut up and go to sleep.'

Casey was outraged. Sleep in a cage ... in his own home, when the bull-pen was across the yard and his own familiar place in the straw was waiting for him. As Liz began to shut the door, he wailed again, and Tich, now certain that something was very wrong, barked loudly, setting off the other animals. This time, Bennie, convinced that intruders had somehow climbed into the farmhouse, began to hurl himself with crashing thumps against the back door, barking more loudly than all the other dogs put together. The shelties flung themselves against the kennel sides, and pushed their noses through the wire mesh of the run, which was used to enclose Nessie when she was in season, and for the dogs at night at other times.

Joe switched on the light again. Casey looked up at him hopefully.

'You fed that damn' cat?' he asked Liz.

'He wants his bull,' Liz said unhappily. It was utterly ridiculous, the way those two animals depended on each other, but what could she do? Seemed strange too when you came to think of it, beyond all reason, yet there were odder partnerships in Zoos, and only the other day she had heard of a racehorse that had to have a billy goat with him wherever he went, even to the races. Daft, animals were. But not much you could do about it when they got one of these fancies.

'I'll put him in the pen,' Joe said at last. He picked up the cage. 'You can sleep in your cage, though, feller. Not as spry as you used to be with that leg.'

The bull was waiting, alone in the dark. His desolate

lows echoed in the yard, but as they approached him, Casey called in greeting and at once was answered. By the time Joe had opened the pen the bull was standing sniffing the air a little uncertainly, for though he could smell the cat he could also smell the antiseptic dressings that had been put on the two puncture holes from the bone splinters, and the odd aftermath of anaesthetic. Ken had used it to mitigate the pain caused by his ministrations.

Joe put the cage down in the straw. The bull settled himself at once. If Casey put his nose through the wire, Sultan could lick it companionably and presently the cat found that he could also put a paw through the mesh and rest it against the bull's hide. Joe heaved a deep sigh. It would be a quiet night after all. Next day was going to be busy.

'O.K.?' Liz asked sleepily as he came into the room.

He nodded, and went to draw the curtains before getting into bed. He liked to be awakened by the first light rather than the alarm clock, not that there was much danger of sleeping through cockcrow, not with the old rooster intent on airing his voice.

Outside moonglow burnished the meadows. He looked across them, across the wide fields and the thick hawthorn hedges, to the shadowy bulk of Fox Wood, lowering against the small rise of the hill. Behind and beyond it the Edge knifed into the sky, with one or two lights still showing from the expensive houses that dotted it. The black bulk of an ancient oak, beyond the cow byres, sheltered a keening owl.

'Hoo. Hoo. Hoo.'

There was a flash of movement and a shape flirted with the moonlight, crossing the ridged shadows, flighting into the gleam and out again, and pounced and flew back again, weighted and heavy, probably with a rat, Joe thought.

He looked down at the yard, at the white run of the fencing, the five-barred gate that led to the road, the bright eyes of a small animal hiding in the bushes, perhaps stoat or weasel, prowling for rat and mouse and shrew and other vermin. Midge was sitting on a fence post, staring at the moon. Bennie lay, a thick shadow among other shadows, only his eyes giving away his hiding place. The dark shapes of cows moved in the meadow, some lying, some grazing, some standing mindless and thoughtless, chewing the cud.

Moonlight glinted on the Bell Brook at the end of the first meadow, its shallows cutting his land in two, running slow and gentle in summer, and in winter and in snowtime, often in spate, rushing brown and turgid, climbing out of its banks and swooping over the flood plain, so that he had to move the beasts, and keep his fingers crossed. The farmhouse had not been flooded since he was a boy, but he could still remember vividly the chaos it caused.

It was strange to look back and remember those days. Remember his mother riding to hounds, first over all the fences, her mocking laugh echoing back to him as he struggled behind on his plump dappled pony ... old Podge. Podge had gone the way of all creatures many years before, but Joe could still remember him, and his odd wicked little temper, his habit of biting when he was tired and unwilling to suffer his grooming, or of nipping suddenly at the hand putting food into his hayrack.

In those days his father had been a big noisy generous active man with a laugh that they could hear from here to the Wheatsheaf, an active hand in all the village affairs, a prominent member of the Liberal party, an outspoken man, a committee member of the local branch of the National Farmers' Union, vocal in all current affairs, a Governor of the local school. It was hard to reconcile him with the man who sat and brooded in the sunny sitting-room, all the valour gone from him after his wife's death. Funny thing, life, Joe thought, as he climbed into bed and caught the fragrance of his wife's hair, and suddenly hugged her to him, grateful for his good fortune, and anxious to show it.

Tich, lying beside the bed, wagged his stump tail, and, one eye open, watched a moth court a moonbeam, soft wings quivering with delight.

CHAPTER ELEVEN

CASEY found convalescence irritating. He had always been an active cat, and his eagerness overcame his disability. Within the week he was trying to walk, standing on three legs; very slowly, carefully, trusting his weight momentarily to the fourth. It was useless trying to cage him. It was painful, and his small gasps haunted Liz, as he spent his days in the kitchen, demanding attention, ready to prove that he could move about, independent of people.

This was not easy. Three paces, four paces, and his strength failed him and he was forced to lie down, an incomprehensible indignity that never failed to draw a fretful wail from him. Midge, who had cast him off long ago and reared another batch of adventurous kittens, had her mother instinct roused again by his helplessness, and spent much of her time lying beside him, her warm tongue licking his healing wounds, bringing comfort.

The dogs were puzzled, but soon came to know that Casey must not be harried or chased or annoyed. Bennie, who had been Casey's main butt and target, missed the games and romps and rough houses, and came one morning into the kitchen to look for the cat. Casey had just discovered that he could no longer open doors with his right paw, as he fell over. He was sitting, baffled, trying to remember how to use his left when the cross-bred Labrador butted the door open, and the cat was knocked backwards with a yell that brought Liz from her desk, where she was making out the milking returns.

Fortunately Casey fell on his uninjured side. He rolled over, and Bennie was upon him, licking the cat's face, his long tail wagging furiously, delighted to find that his sparring partner was still around and able to greet him. Casey, lying on his back under the onslaught, protested by raking one hind leg beneath the dog, showing his disapproval. The useless leg refused to co-operate, and Bennie, aware that there was something wrong, flopped to the ground beside the cat and lay there with his tail thumping heavily on the stone floor, and a benign expression on his always friendly face.

It was not like Bennie to come into the house during the day, and Liz, seeing an unfamiliar vehicle draw up in the yard, looked at the dog, wondering if he were about to neglect his guard duties. Not Bennie. He heard the wheels skid on the cobbles, and left the cat and greeted the newcomer with harsh angry barks that kept the driver in his seat.

'Horse for yer, missus,' he shouted, above the din. Liz yelled to Bennie, who was making up for his neglect by an unusual amount of noise. Casey, intrigued, limped to the doorway, and flopped in a patch of sunlight, anxious to miss nothing. Watching the outside world had become his major occupation and he was concerned to find out everything that happened, often asking Liz to place him on the wide windowsill, where he could look out in comfort, following her, painfully slowly, wailing, until she realized his need and obeyed his demands.

Bennie, convinced at last that this was part of the farm

business, even though both vehicle and driver were completely strange, sat with his bulk leaning against the high doorstep, within reach of the cat. He was hot. Running around the lorry barking was exhausting work. He panted noisily, ready to interfere if the intruder showed any threatening sign at all.

The lorry driver, a small man with a shock of white hair that was vivid in contrast to his sunburnt face, jumped nimbly from the cab and opened the door at the back of the truck. He lowered the ramp, and Liz stared as a honey coloured mare stepped down, her expression scornful. She tossed her head, and danced a few paces, and then whinnied, turning in astonishment as there came an eager scuffle from the stallion's loose-box and a roar of welcome.

Hastily, Liz closed the half-door, shutting Starlight into the dark, where he vented his displeasure by kicking a hind hoof thunderously against the wooden partition. The mare waited. She was nervous, her ears flattened, and her eyes whitened. Liz approached, conscious of the long trembling legs and the fact that the beast was unhappy, among strangers, in unfamiliar surroundings. Liz clucked to her, but she was having none of it. She turned away her head.

'Hoo's a beauty!' Lew had come from the field, where he had been overlooking the cattle. One of the heifers had broken through a gap in the hedge, and he had put her back and counted the remainder, and then closed the breach with old timbers that Joe had bought from a disused railway line. Came in handy.

His hand went to the sleek neck, his face was within inches of the anxious head, and then the mare sighed and relaxed. Lew was safety, he smelled good, and she trusted him. Meekly, she let him take her head rope and lead her into the loose-box that he and Nat had prepared for her. The foal, now free in the field on the other side of the yard, stopped in his cavortings, skidded to a standstill and stared with baby curiosity at this stranger, and Candy, jealous at the sight of another mare, nosed him away from the gate. When he refused and stood stockstill, she butted him and then nipped his neck, so that he broke away from her with a whinny and galloped over to stand beneath the tree and stare with reproachful eyes. Candy, satisfied, nuzzled him in apology.

Casey watched the mare with interest. The strangest things happened in his world. One day there would be a cow in the end byre, and next day there would be three beasts, and the cow would angle a horn at him when he went to explore, while the smaller beasts watched him with curious eyes. He did not stay long. He disliked the smell of new calves, an odd sweetish smell that almost choked him.

He had been equally mystified when Midge had her second litter of kittens, finding his half brothers and sisters most surprising creatures at first. He had nosed them as they lay helpless in the box, blind and squealing, moving minute paws restlessly, and had then learned to stay away as Midge gave him a lashing with her clawed forepaw, marking his head with deep scratches that marred his nose and just missed the eye. Not till the kittens were old enough to wander did Casey see them again, and then he had found them wonderful companions, always ready for a romp in the straw in the big barn.

They had not stayed long. The littlest one had stepped unwisely beneath Starlight's hooves, and the others all had gone to new homes. Casey missed them.

Now there was another beast to discover. When his leg behaved again. He stood up, wondering if he could follow Lew, but it was all too much for him. The angry twinge that tore at the broken bone and damaged muscles forced him to sit again, staring up at Liz with sorrowful eyes.

'Poor old boy,' she said, and brought him a spoonful of cream on a saucer, a rare and unparalleled treat. He licked at it dubiously and then, realizing that here was nectar, settled his face over the saucer and lapped blissfully. Finished, he licked at the aftertaste, his pink tongue cleaning every whisker and hair, and then limped painfully to paw at Liz's leg and beg for sanctuary on her lap, which she never denied him, his legs against her, his front paws and nose overlapping her knees, while he throbbed his gratitude, sighed, washed one paw with quick savagery, and then fell into a deep sleep. He had walked eleven paces that morning. It had been quite exhausting.

By the end of a fortnight the mare knew Liz, and she also knew Casey. The cat was fascinated by her, and often came to sit in the patch of sunshine beside her stable, and watch her, as she watched him. She was not sure of him, but he intrigued her, and her quick ears thrust forward when he wailed, ready to catch the least sound. She was even more interested when Tartar came visiting and father and son kept up a long series of strange noises, which always made Liz and Lew sure that they were conversing.

Casey began to follow Liz about. She had to carry him upstairs at first, when she went to make the beds and tidy up, otherwise he sat on the bottom stair and howled until she took pity on him. Once upstairs he limped slowly after her, pausing frequently to rest his leg, and then trying his weight on it again, one, two, three, and hobble, with a slow and awkward gait that Liz found most upsetting.

One morning she forgot him, and was startled to hear a strange noise on the stairs. She looked down. Casey had reached the fifth stair. Left forepaw. Right forepaw. A deep breath, and then an astounding bunny hop, coming up with both hind legs together. He paused for a long rest and she went to lift him, but he protested, and, afraid that he would fall, she left him, and watched as he jumped towards her, each stair an achievement, a milestone in his recovery, and one, moreover, that the cat himself regarded as significant.

After that, he practised stair climbing, becoming more and more proficient, but continuing to bound up with both hind legs together in an ungainly series of jumps, landing so noisily it sounded as if he was coming through the treads. Coming down was another matter, and quite beyond him, so that Liz found herself carrying him down again, only to discover that he had once more made his way to the top and was yelling for rescue.

By the time that the two fell ponies arrived, Casey could circumnavigate the yard, exclaiming loudly all the time, plainly overcome by his own progress. His calls were punctuated by the bull's replies, and although Liz felt no more affection for the beast, she was amused by the ridiculous sound of pseudo-conversation, question in loud yowl and reply in a shrill low that sounded absurd coming from so big an animal.

By the time Tartar had strolled in and added his own comments to the conference even passers-by were entertained and leaned on the gate in the sunshine to watch Casey limping from place to place, and practise jumping, an accomplishment that it was necessary to learn all over again as his right hind leg was now an inch shorter than the left and when he jumped he was unbalanced.

Several times Liz found him in the sitting-room, jumping from chair to chair, as if unable to find a comfortable spot to rest in. Until she noticed that each time he landed he slipped and fell sideways, and that each jump corrected this, until at last he could once more gauge his distance, and land erect, whereupon he sat with an inane expression of pure pleasure on his small whiskered face, and then began to wash assiduously, tugging at the fur between his paws, making up for the days on which he had felt too weary and disinclined to attempt such a thorough toilet.

He was wary of the horses. Each night he crept back to his place beside the bull, lying there, his purr filling the air, while Sultan made a peculiar crooning groan that sounded like an imitation of the cat's throb, and sent Lew and Nat into chuckles every time they heard it.

Liz had no time left for brooding. The mare and the two ponies and Candy and her foal were her concern, and the Fenton children appeared to have taken up residence. Nat came in daily, delighted to be with horses again, and refusing any payment for his services, afraid that it would affect his pension. Liz paid him in kind in the end, rather than argue, so that he took home a weekly supply of eggs, milk, butter, and an occasional chicken, making Rosie happier than she had been for years, as she found meat in her pantry and pennies left in her purse at the end of the week.

Mike Flynn was another regular. He had taken over Starlight for Joe and kept the big hunter exercised, which was a blessing for everyone, as his long treks every day not only kept him fit, but kept him placid. Liz had always been afraid that Joe, riding the horse after a break of a week or more, would be thrown. Starlight was both determined and frisky when he'd a mind.

He liked Mike, who had a way with horses and a knack of understanding them, thinking like the horse as he rode him, watching the flickering ears for telltales, so that he knew as soon as the horse did that there was a man taking a quick drag in the shelter of a tree, a man who might move astonishingly and suddenly, or another man half hidden in the foliage of the ditch, with a scythe that would flash blindingly and frighteningly. His firm hand and soft voice were always ready to soothe and gentle, to reassure, telling the horse that tractors could not hurt, that lorries were intent on keeping to their own side of the road, and not at all likely to break away and charge him, that the flashing scythe offered him no harm, that the man behind the tree was not going to move. The warning was for the man as much as for the beast. Countrymen stayed still and never flapped an arm when horses were near, but townsfolk often did not realize how nervous the beasts were, and many a driver, coming too close, left a cavorting horse and unnerved rider behind him, having terrified the animal with the noise of the monster he was driving and the bewildering and uncanny screech of its gears. No use trying to explain to the horse. He couldn't understand.

During the weeks that followed Mike took all the ponies in hand in turn. This was his element, and he loved schooling them, taming them, gentling them, as he had trained and tamed the big police horses that had been in his care when he was Inspector. No use looking back. Only forward, and his wife was delighted to see him put on weight again, regain the colour in his cheeks and the brightness in his eyes, and talk with enthusiasm of the horses at Wayman's Corner. Like Nat, he was not interested in payment, but Liz kept him supplied with farm produce too, and his pension stretched much further than he had ever imagined it could, relieved of the need to pay for milk and eggs and the occasional side of bacon.

Casey found a new allegiance, and followed Mike, his small paws pit patting behind, limp, limp, limp, but faster now and always determined not to be forgotten or left behind. He kept well clear of the ponies. Candy's kick had taught him a lesson that he would never forget.

'What are you going to call them?' Jane demanded, wolfing farm bread and fresh butter and honey from Liz's two hives. She had grown in the past months and her dress was too short and tight, her pigtails half braided, her tanned small face dirty. Home was not a friendly place just now. Her mother was often irritable, hating the country and regretting the town, and averse to animals. Frogs invading the kitchen sent her into a panic; Tartar's frequent dead birds and mice upset her beyond all measure, so that she smacked the cat, who now had only to see her to turn his tail to her, and race away, usually taking refuge at the farm where he became a more and more frequent visitor. Peter did not notice his mother's irritation, but it upset Jane, who came to Liz for comfort, which Liz gave in full measure without even being aware that it was demanded or necessary.

'Call the horses?' Liz had not had time to think. 'Let's go and think of names now,' she suggested, and Jane caught her hand, and tugged her through the scullery, across the cobbled yard and to the field where the mare and the two geldings were grazing. Candy was in the far field. Any horse approaching her foal was either kicked or bitten, and not unnaturally, this was resented, so that the mare had landed a well aimed kick and one of the fell ponies had bitten back.

Jane climbed on to the second rung of the five-barred gate and looked at the animals thoughtfully. The mare came for her titbits. Liz always had carrots in her pockets. The ponies had not yet accepted her and watched suspiciously, from the far side of the field.

'She's Honey,' Jane said with satisfaction, watching the sun gild the golden hide. 'Honey's a pretty name, isn't it?' she asked, suddenly afraid that Liz might say, as her mother so often did, 'Don't be silly!'

'Suits her down to her hooves,' Liz agreed. It was an easy simple name. 'Here's another carrot, Honey,' she said, and the mare took it greedily, and then tossed her mane and galloped across the field, knowing that no more would be forthcoming.

The fell ponies were both rolling in the long grass, revelling in the feel of the sun on their hides, kicking their hooves like colts. Candy's foal, seeing them, followed suit.

'I think they ought to be called Jack and Jill,' Jane said.

'They're both boys, stupid.' Peter had come running towards them, his knees and hands filthy, after trying to catch the little frogs in the pond.

'Jack and Sprat.'

'That's daft.' Peter was superior. He sat on the top bar of the gate and tried to whistle, a feat that proved unusually difficult as he had a gap in his front teeth, which were very widely spaced.

Jane looked as if she was about to cry. Life was getting too difficult. Peter teased and Mummy was always cross, and even Daddy got grumpy and never listened to her. She clutched Liz's hand tighter, so that Liz looked down with a faintly worried expression, wondering why the child seemed so anxious and edgy these days.

The fell ponies were half-brothers, both fathered by the same sire. They had been reared together, only a week apart in age, and now stood with the sun gilding their dappled coats, one resting his head across the other's muscular neck.

The foal cantered in front of them, on the other side of the gate, kicking up his neat hind hooves engagingly. He yickered, teasing them, asking them to race across the meadow, to chase beside him and help him develop his muscles, ready for his adult life. One pony dipped his head, and tossed his mane; the other ducked and bucked and snorted. The three of them began to run, savouring the teasing wind that thrust inquiring fingers through mane and tail. Lew, bringing buckets of additional feed for them, and the foal's ration of extra milk, for now he was almost weaned, and Candy was dry again, stood and watched them, an amused grin on his face.

'Pitch 'n toss,' he said to Jane, as one of the ponies bucked again and the other flung up its head and the long mane tossed in the breeze.

'Those are lovely names,' Jane said excitedly. 'That one's Pitch, who keeps bucking. And that one's Toss. He keeps tossing.'

'They're silly names.' Peter had no intention of agreeing with his sister. Silly little kid. Couldn't even whistle.

'They're nice names.' Jane looked anxiously at Liz.

'They're just right.' Liz looked at the ponies. It was never easy to find reasonable names. Honey, Pitch and Toss solved the problem very well.

'Candy's foal is going to be called Baby,' Jane said, as the tiny creature came towards her inquisitively, and stood, all four hooves planted firmly together, his big eyes looking her over, intensely curious. He saw Lew come into the field and charged towards him, eager to get at the bucket. Soon his small head was deep inside it and the children were chuckling over the intensely greedy sucking noises that he made as he drank.

'Baby's a silly name. He'll be bigger 'n Candy one day. He ought to be called Guzzler,' Peter announced.

'Guzzler.' Lew grinned at the thought, and Liz suddenly knew that no matter how they named the foal, he would certainly be called Guzzler by everybody.

'I think Shadow's a nice name for him,' Jane said. The foal's coat was darkening. Liz guessed that his father had been a very dark bay. Shadow would suit him admirably. He lifted his head, milk sprinkling his nostrils, and suddenly snuffled, spraying Lew with white drops.

'Guzzler!' said Peter, and stalked off to tease Tartar and smooth Casey's coat. Casey had limped over to the field with them and was sitting beside them, waving an offended tail, staring jealously at the horses. He wanted Liz to notice him, to stoop down, and pick him up and comfort him, but he was not going to plead for attention.

'Casey, you'll just have to lie in the manger and watch me,' Liz said, scratching the cat under his chin. He looked up at her, narrowing his eyes. Nessie, sitting to scratch frantically at an itching shoulder, suddenly became jealous too, and rolled over. Liz rubbed her tummy with the toe of her shoe and Nessie thumped her tail on the cobblestones.

That evening, when Mike Flynn came to help with the ponies, he brought his whippet bitch. Shanie kept close to his heels, afraid of other dogs and of the giant horses that seemed to move their long clumsy legs so casually. She cowered in a corner of the stable as the ponies were brought in.

'How would you like to ride Candy home, and I'll lead her back again?' Liz asked Jane.

Jane nodded her head, and went to look for the saddle.

'I'm worried about that child,' Liz said, frowning, as she saddled Honey. Mike, busy with Starlight, spoke over his shoulder.

'There's gossip,' he said. 'Not going to repeat it. But I fancy there's trouble brewing. Honest to God,' he said savagely, under his breath so as not to alarm the hunter, 'you'd think people would have more sense.'

Liz did not answer. Jill came less and less often to the farm, and when she did her talk was wistful; of city life and parties and pretty clothes and witty people, everything so far removed from Liz's own orbit that it was almost impossible to understand. Paul, during the last few weeks, had been brusque when he came to collect Tartar and on many occasions the Siamese had departed for home alone, complaining bitterly, as he considered it his prerogative to be fetched, and to accompany his master in the walk home, appearing suddenly and mysteriously from behind hedges, crossing in front of Paul, and occasionally rolling in the dust, calling attention to himself, asking for affection. The farm was fun, but it was not home, and Tartar scorned to demand affection from Liz. She belonged to Midge and Casey.

The ponies turned quietly into the lane. Jane was ecstatic. She loved riding Candy, loved the feel of the pony's neck beneath her hands, and the ecstasy that overwhelmed her when she began to trot and could at last synchronize her movements with the pony's. There was nothing quite like it in the whole world, no sense of achievement that could compare, and also nothing that could equal her high-up view, looking down on the unfamiliar things about her, so different when seen from above, and not from a child's height. Most of all, she liked to look down at her father, seeing him as other adults saw him.

Liz rode Honey, while Mike came behind on Starlight, flagging down cars that came too fast or too close. At the edge of the road, keeping to the grass verge, came Tich, his busy nose sniffing at any hole and burrow. Casey, able to limp along, stumbled after them, eyes alert, watching for mice in the hedgerow, and chattering in fury at birds that dared to fly too near him, and Tartar came too, his tail stiff, his voice delightedly telling the world that here he was, out for a walk with horses. Me, Tartar. And horses. He seemed unable to get over it, and both Liz and Jane laughed at him so that he cast one offended look over his shoulder and walked with dignity through a gap in the hedge.

His dignity suffered a speedy shock. The field was full of heifers, frisky and unmanaged, and one of them charged towards him so that he shot backwards into the lane, proclaiming his outrage.

'He is silly,' Jane said, looking at the cat as he ran in front of them, still shouting. Casey, interested, followed him, lagleg dragging, occasionally adding comments of his own, and Tich wagged his stump tail and plodded on, always pleased to be with the cats.

A breeze ruffled the hedge tops and stirred the guardian trees. A blackbird flew, scolding, and three magpies sprang from a coppice and glided over the field. One of them alighted near a small flock of birds. Jane, turning her head, saw the greedy beak stab at a sparrow, heard the scolding as the flock scattered, and cried out in dismay as the black and white bird flapped heavily towards a stark, lightning stripped birch that lifted scarecrow branches out of the hedgerow.

'Beastly thing,' Jane said, almost crying.

'They have to live,' Mike told her, riding alongside. 'The sparrow died fast.'

It was poor reassurance but it was the best he could do. He remembered his battles with his own son long ago, about eating sheep and cows. Terry had been a vegetarian for years before he overcame that prejudice. Too many things in life that you couldn't reconcile, like cancer, and cholera, and it didn't do to think of things like war and famine and earthquakes. Just had to take it as you could and shrug it off as best you could, or life would be intolerable.

'Home,' he said, and lifted Jane down. She left them at once and ran into the house crying 'Mummy, Mummy.' Liz waited till she heard Jill's voice. But no voice answered. The child's cries grew shriller, and she came flying into the garden again, and grabbed Liz's leg so tightly that the stirrup cut into her ankle.

'There isn't no one there!'

Mike took Honey's reins, and Liz went back into the house. It was clean and tidy, every room neat, the kitchen spotless, but no sign of a meal, which Jill would normally have been preparing.

'Her car isn't there,' Jane said, coming back from the garage. 'She didn't say she wouldn't be here.'

'Let's leave a note,' Liz said, finding pencil and paper. 'Then you come back with me and we'll make a special supper party for Uncle Joe and you can help me feed the horses and get them ready for the night.'

'I don't want to ride,' Jane said. Somehow all the savour had gone from that particular adventure. 'I want to walk back.'

'You come up on Starlight,' Mike said. His firm arms enfolded her, reassuring and safe. She leaned against the solid comfort of his body, intrigued to find she was even higher above the world on Starlight's back. The hunter quivered his ears, wary, because this was unusual, but Mike stood no nonsense from any horse, and the beast knew it. He was meek as a new fledged sparrow as he walked back to Wayman's Corner.

The small retinue of followers, tired now, returned as quietly. Tartar, finding no people in his own place, was coming back with his friends, anxious not to be on his own. He hated that more than anything in the world. He needed people and other animals to talk to, and his small voice grumbled all the time, in a smothered undertone, if he were ever alone.

Peter met them at the gate.

'Mummy's not there,' Jane said. She began to cry. 'I wish I knew where she is.'

Liz lifted the child down and took her indoors, while Mick unsaddled the horses. The clock ticked insistently, emphasizing her worries.

'I wish I knew where she is.'

The phrase became irritating. Jane said it over and over again, as if it held some magic quality, some reassurance, that saying it often enough would bring its own answer.

'I wish you'd shut up,' Peter said. He felt sick. His middle had gone into a small tight knot and there was another knot in his throat. He had a vivid imagination, and saw his mother lying under a car, or worse, trapped in her own, or in a burning building shouting for help. He would be there, big and brave, calling to her and would rescue her. He soothed himself with his own anodyne, but Jane's small plea came more frequently, as the hours went by, and they ate supper with one eye on the door, and sat uneasily, no longer feeling welcome, but intruders, there unusually, although Liz tried to reassure them and played a long and painful game of Rummy with Jane and listened for the telephone, and watched the window into the yard, and waited for a car. Jill's car, Paul's car, a police car, any car.

'Where is Mummy?' Jane asked for the hundredth time. 'Do you think she'll ever come home?'

And Liz, recognizing the question that had been in her own heart, was suddenly chilled. She picked the child up in her arms and held her close, kissing the blonde head.

'Why don't you tell me?' Jane was overtired and fretful, long past bedtime, hating the unfamiliar. But Liz had no reply at all. What could be the answer? She only wished she knew.

CHAPTER TWELVE

THE children were in bed in the spare room. Liz had been up to them twice in the past hour. Jane, bewildered and unhappy, had sobbed herself to sleep, but Peter lay, stony-faced, dry-eyed, watching the moonlight creep slim-fingered across the unfamiliar floor. He dared not think about his parents any more. His mother had gone. His father would have telephoned. If they'd been all right. So they weren't all right, and he lay there saying his tables over and over. Twice one is two. Twice two is four. It was better than thinking, better than worrying and wondering, better than nothing. Casey had curled up on Jane's bed. Tartar lay beside Peter, and the cat was consolation. Peter stroked the soft fur, and as the rich even purr resounded the tears that he had been keeping in check spilled over, angering him. Liz, outside the door, hearing a small sob, went downstairs again. She could do nothing for him and he would hate her to see him cry.

Joe had twice driven back to the Fentons' house and the last time had locked it securely. It was not wise to leave it open after dark. Paul, returning, would guess what had happened. Restless, he went out to the horses, and stood talking to Starlight, who rubbed his head against his master, overjoyed by the rare attention. Sultan, lonely, called for Casey, and presently Liz heard the cat's steps, flip flop, stip stop, coming unevenly down the stairs. It was surprising how fast he could move, but the limp was dreadful, his whole body slip sliding sideways as he walked. His raucous mew was answered eagerly by the bull's weirder low, a sound reserved for Casey, and soon he was curled beside the beast and sound asleep again.

When Peter at last fell asleep, Tartar, as if released from a duty, left him, and came downstairs, and sat staring at Liz, as if asking her why they were all there and not at home. She rubbed the side of his head with her finger nail, and most unusually, he jumped on to her lap and lay there, still regarding her with that wide blue cross-eyed unwinking stare.

'I dunno,' Joe said, putting the kettle on to boil. 'Ought to do something. Dunno where to start.'

'Police?' Liz suggested. 'Something must be wrong. They'd never leave the children.'

Joe went to the telephone. He sat, staring at the dial, and then picked up the receiver and began to spin out the number. Luckily he knew the sergeant well.

'Sounds a queer do,' the sergeant said, when he heard the story. 'I don't quite know where to begin, and that's a fact, but I'll see what I can do. They might 'ave gone anywhere.'

'Both cars are out,' Joe said.

There seemed nothing more to say. He made the tea, and poured it, and cut a slice of fruit cake, and then began to pace the kitchen, noting with half an eye that the stitching on Candy's saddle was wearing, that the hunter needed a new girth, that the clock needed winding.

'Honey's in foal,' Liz said. 'Did they tell you when you bought her?'

Joe shook his head, only half his mind on Liz. He

wished he could get the car and go looking for the Fentons though heavens only knew where. Those two poor little devils . . . if there was no news by morning—

'Can't do much good sitting here,' Liz said at last. There was an extension to the telephone beside her bed. 'We'd better get some sleep.'

She went upstairs. Tartar, more bewildered than ever, followed her, and sat on the windowsill watching the night while she undressed. Once she was in bed he went to her, and pushed his head against her hand, over and over again, as if begging for reassurance.

Joe locked the stables, putting a last ration of hay in each rack. He spoke to Starlight before he left, and gentled Honey, and Candy's foal, looked at the sleeping cows, relieved to see no sign of trouble among them. Several calves were due, but the cattle were quiet enough tonight. No sign of imminent birth. The humped trees hid some of them from him. No need to go and look. He knew the telltales.

Bennie was on guard in the yard, his wise eyes watchful. His tail thudded as Joe bent to stroke him, and he lay, nose on paws, watching for movement, listening for strangers. A car whined up the lane, changed gear, and was gone. An owl called, soft whoo whooing, and drifted past on a thread of noise. Grass rustled and Midge pounced and went off, proud-footed, carrying a mouse. The church clock struck one. Time indeed to be a-bed. Joe stood at the white five-barred gate, looking down the lane to the wide spread of the church green. The spire was dark against the sky. The church had stood there, brooding over the village, while men had come and gone and kings had died and other kings succeeded them, and wars had split the earth and millions had suffered from flood and fire and famine, war and pestilence and

145

earthquake. The one thing all men shared was sorrow. Pity it had to start so young.

He climbed the stairs without his boots, treading softly on the bare oak, and peeped in through the open spare room door. The moon angled across Jane's small face, her hair spread on the pillow, finespun silk, and Peter, even in sleep his face sulky, moved restlessly.

'Damn Paul Fenton,' Joe thought savagely as he undressed in the dark, aware that Tartar was watching him. 'Don't his children mean a thing to him ... surely he could have sent a message ... some message ... and here are Liz and I ...'

He did not often think of his own son lying dead on the hill, but the thought came now to tease and torment, so that he was wide awake when the telephone bell savaged the silence, and took the thing off its stand at once, aware of Liz, leaning on one elbow, staring at him, only her eyes visible in the gloom.

'We'll keep the children till we hear something else,' he said at last, and rang off.

'What is it?' Liz had crept close to him. He could feel her trembling.

'Jill came out of a side road into the main road near Bristol this afternoon and was hit by a petrol tanker. Paul's been with her all night.'

'Is she ...?'

'Yes.'

Joe turned his back and lay looking at the night sky through the window square. He had no comfort to offer, no words that were worth saying, and he was dreading the morning and the children's questions and the news that they would have to give. And what was Jill doing in Bristol, nearly two hundred miles away?

The church clock struck two. And three. And four, and

146

at four thirty it was light enough to pretend he had extra chores to do and to dress, and go downstairs, and let the dogs out, and take a gun and go striding over the dew wet fields, where the first birds shouted as if day had never dawned before or would again.

Nat was helping Lew with the milking when Joe came back, two rabbits hanging head down from his hand. He swung them by their paws, not seeing them. He listened uneasily before he went through into the kitchen, but there was no sound of children's voices.

He walked into a silence that seemed to have been going on for ever. Mike Flynn was standing by the big oak dresser, his fingers tracing the round edge of a handle, over and over again, while Liz, Tartar against her leg, and Casey on her shoulder, his paws dangling, stood facing him, her face drawn and white, and the police sergeant, his own face grey with weariness, his eyes sickened, stood with a sheet of paper in his hands, screwing it into nothing.

'Joe,' Liz said, and stopped.

Mike Flynn cleared his throat.

'Mr. Fenton left the hospital in Bristol early this morning, to come home,' he said. 'He had arranged to go back tomorrow . . . to see about the funeral, and all that.'

The clock chimed, and Joe was conscious of its solemn tick, of the bull, petulant, stamping and lowing in his pen, presage of a bad day, of the movements of the children in the room above, presumably as they dressed.

'He took his car along the motorway. And accelerated into the pillar of a bridge.'

Liz left the room. It was more than she could bear. She ran outside into Honey's stable, and busied herself savagely, tedding hay and measuring rations, while Honey nosed her delicately as if aware that she needed comfort.

The men stared at one another. Nat, from the doorway, spoke into the stillness.

'Not the kind of man that ever faced up to things, Mr. Fenton.'

It was a statement of plain fact, to Nat's mind. He always saw clearly. To Joe, it was also an epitaph.

The children came into the room. Mike looked at Joe, and the sergeant nodded brusquely and went outside. He had been at the scene of many crashes but he was still sickened. He hated cowardice and to his mind this was the worst kind of all. To leave the bairns to face life alone . . .

'Come and help wi' milking,' Nat said, holding out a hand to Jane. She took it trustingly, and Peter followed her, tasting the atmosphere in the quiet kitchen and finding fear in it.

'How in hell do we tell them?' Joe asked when they had gone. He took his whip from the wall and slashed at the floor with it, the quick swickering sound helping to relieve pent feelings.

Mike Flynn shrugged. He had no comfort either, and the two men went outside, and were startled to hear Lew's voice, talking to the children.

'It were all over quick, and your Mam's in Heaven. Her's happy, see, and yer Dad too, that way, both on 'em's together. And you'll be here wi' Mr. Wayman and Mis' Liz. They haven't got no little 'uns, so that's all fine and good for them too.'

Liz, hearing him, buried her face in Honey's neck, and dared not move it when Jane crept in to her, and caught at her hand. They stood together, comforting one another, with Honey's muzzle thrust between them, and Honey's gold head rubbing against them. When at last they dried their eyes and went out into the sunlit yard, it was to find Mike cantering in the field on Starlight, with Peter held in front of him in the saddle, and Joe, unusually busy in the kitchen, grilling more bacon than they could ever eat, adding rasher after rasher, as if the mere act of cooking could blot out thought. Nat had come inside and laid the table, and was walking round the kitchen talking to the animals, who, too long unfed, were whining and weaving, asking over and over again for their meal.

'Will we stay with you?' Jane asked, her mouth full of egg and bacon. Grief seemed to have sharpened her appetite rather than removed it.

'I hope so, love,' Liz said.

'I'll go straight after I've eaten and find out . . . have you any aunts and uncles or grandparents?' Joe asked.

Peter shook his head.

'Mummy and Daddy were both onlies . . .' Peter said. 'And Granny Fenton got married to somebody else and went to America; and that's all of us there are.'

'I don't want to go to America,' Jane said. 'I want to live here. With Honey and Candy and the pigs and the cats and the chickens and the ducks . . .' She was talking to hide her fears, Liz decided, as the child began to prattle endlessly, a spate of words that filled each silence.

No one mentioned school. Peter helped to muck out the stables, to feed the pigs and take the cows back to the meadow. He helped scrub out an empty stable so that when Honey had her foal there was a special foaling place for her; he creosoted the top fence.

Jane fed the chickens and fetched the eggs and helped carry hay bales. When work was done, Liz invented more, anything to fill the time and tire the child, and keep her from thinking. In the afternoon Lew took the children over to Mike Flynn, whose wife had prepared a special tea, a party tea, with savoury sandwiches and a big iced cake, and sausage rolls and gingerbread men with icing sugar faces. While they were away Liz phoned the school and explained to the horrified teacher.

'Better keep them away for a day or two,' she said. 'The other children are sure to discuss it. . . . I've never heard such a terrible thing.'

Liz made some reply and rang off. It was not going to be easy to cope with people. They meant well, but whatever they said was wrong. And supposing Joe did unearth some other relations? She wanted the children more than she had ever wanted anything in the world, and the sudden savagery of her feelings frightened her.

Casey, hungry again, howled at her in disgust, and she started once more on the endless round, feeding the dogs and cats, the pigs and chickens and horses. Good job the cows could feed themselves in summer, she thought idiotically, as she took the bottle out to a calf that Joe had bought at the last Beast Sale. She longed for the phone to ring, for Joe to tell her what had happened. But when at last the bell summoned her from the yard, she was afraid to answer it.

CHAPTER THIRTEEN

NOTHING was simple in the next few weeks. There were formalities, all endless. Inquiries to be made, arrangements for the inquests, and then the nightmare began.

Nat came in with the local paper, banner headlines screaming.

'I can't read it,' Liz said.

'You'd best, Mis' Liz. You'd best know.' Nat's voice was thick and angry.

Liz took the paper. Joe had been to the inquest, while she had stayed with the children. He had come home silent, said nothing all evening, and gone off the next day with only a brusque word to her. She was totally unprepared for what she read.

Nat whistled between his teeth, a thin reedy infuriating note. The children were helping Lew. Jane had become bored with work, and was dragging a string across the yard. Casey, delighted, was pouncing and pulling, biting and teasing, overjoyed by the constant presence of a playmate who always had time for him. Liz was half-conscious of his absurd antics, but her brain refused to believe what her eyes read.

'It's not true,' she said at last.

'Too true, Mis' Liz. I never said, not being a gossip, like. Her's off every day wi' that young man as was killed wi' her. Too pretty for her own good, Mis' Jill. Reckon

Mr. Fenton knew, all along. Couldn't do owt. There's allus some like that. Had a bitch once, proper flighty her was, wouldn't even feed her pups. Went off gadding. Nowt to be done wi' 'em. And in 'umans, it don't make for happiness.'

'We can't let the children go back to school ... not this term ... and what about the village? They mustn't know ... but how can we keep it from them?' Liz felt sick. She had never suspected anything. Suddenly she found herself wondering, thinking about other people she knew, afraid to think too hard unless under the familiar surface she saw a stranger, unless under the proffered friendship she found enmity, unless behind the everyday façade there was something so alien that it left her terrified.

'Village won't talk. Nobody 'd hurt t' kids. But best not let them go to school. Other kids won't be so careful.'

Mike Flynn put his head round the door.

'You've seen it,' he said heavily.

Liz nodded.

'Mike, did you know?'

'I knew. Knew some and guessed the rest.' His voice was sombre. 'Been the talk at the Wheatsheaf for long enough now.'

'How could she?' Liz asked, looking out at Jane, who was romping in the hay with Casey and Tartar, both playing the fool, all of them mad with sunshine and excitement. Tich barked at them, his body angled, front legs bent, so that his head was close to the ground, and Bennie, busy watching the gate, absentmindedly thudded his tail. It was all so safe, so familiar, that she clutched the reality, pushing away the thought of Jill's infidelities, not just one, but many of them, for as long as they had known her.

'She hated the country. Uprooted from everything she knew,' Mike said. 'Hated animals too, and the loneliness. She was such a pretty little thing, dainty and needed fun and a lot of attention. No use putting her down in the middle of a field and hoping she'd settle. Like a bird . . . she had to try her wings. Flew too high, poor soul.'

'Nowt to do but face it,' Nat said. 'And then forget. Kids are alive. Let what's dead stay dead. Fowk forget. Nine days wonder, and then no more. Coom a big bit o' news, and no one'll remember. Better get on wi' chores,' Nat added. He stuffed tobacco into his disreputable old pipe and went out to stand and contemplate the pigs, prior to mucking out.

Jane was running across the yard. Mike picked up the newspaper and pocketed it, and turned with a smile for her as she flew into the kitchen, and grabbed Liz's hand.

'Midge has got more kittens. In a big box in the stable. Come and see. Four kittens, black and white and one all white, and d'you think Tartar is the daddy cat? They've got their eyes shut tight . . . like this . . .' she demonstrated, and Liz gave Mike a half-smile, thanking Heaven that children were so easily distracted. He, thinking of the talk last night at the Wheatsheaf, where the evening paper had been bandied around, giving all the details about the inquest, followed them outside.

It was cool and dim in the stables. Starlight looked out over his half door, and Honey rested sleepily in her loose-box. The coming foal was visible now, the mare's sleek shape a receding memory. She greeted them with a soft whinny.

Midge mewed.

'Look,' Jane said, and knelt to watch as the almost new kits fed, moving paper thin claws. 'Their paws are so tiny. Can I hold one?'

'Not yet,' Liz said. 'Midge doesn't like anyone touching her babies till they can walk. Then you can.'

'Will they walk tomorrow.'

'Not for a week or two yet,' Mike said, and went outside as the lorry drew up for the churns.

'Right old goings-on in your village,' Bert Taylor shouted, humping the first churn into the back of the lorry.

'Shut up,' Mike hissed.

'Not one of her stars, were you?' Bert asked, his teeth brilliant in his reddened face, his eyes mocking.

'The Fenton children are living with me,' Liz said, suddenly furious. She had liked Bert up to now, and she hated him at this moment.

He looked at her, shame-faced.

'I didn't know,' he mumbled, and swung the remaining churns aboard and swung out into the lane.

'Hateful man,' Liz said furiously, and stormed into the kitchen, her colour high. For the next half hour she vented her rage on the dishes.

She was startled by the sound of the milk lorry returning.

'Oh no,' she thought, having almost forgotten Bert in the interval that had elapsed since his departure. She looked outside, and was relieved to see Peter helping Lew with the far fence, which Cherry had broken in the night, trying to reach the longer grass in the ditch, and Jane trotting happily on Candy, beside Mike, who was walking Starlight.

Bert came sheepishly into the kitchen.

'I'm sorry, Mrs. Wayman. I didn't know. Poor little devils. Look, I got these for 'em. And some ice-cream.'

He dumped the cartons on the table, and put a box down beside them. His face redder than ever, he hurried out to the lorry and revved his engine, making Bennie bark. Liz, blank-faced, watched him turn out into the lane, and then shook her head. People were completely incomprehensible.

He had brought enough ice-cream for an army of children. Liz smiled to herself as she put it away in the refrigerator, and looked inside the box. Two budgerigars crouched there forlornly, and she remembered suddenly that Bert had an aviary. She went to find the cage that had been lying, for as long as she could remember, in the attic, and when the children came in to their lunch, the two birds were feeding on the seed that Bert had put in with them.

'Those are yours. Bert, the milkchurn man, gave them to you,' Liz told them.

'All our very own? Not a bit yours too?' Jane asked.

'All your own. You can feed them, and clean out the cage for them if you want to,' Liz said, knowing perfectly well that in the end this would be yet another chore for her.

'Mine's the greeny one and yours is the bluey one,' Jane said, putting her finger through the bars. Her budgerigar nipped her. 'I'll call you Nipper, you horrid thing.'

'I'll call mine Fred,' Peter decided. He called most of his possessions Fred. His Teddy bear and an old and battered toy dog, neither of which he owned to possessing, but neither of which could be thrown away, were both also called Fred.

The days were not so bad as the nights. Peter showed no sign of disturbance, but Jane, as soon as she was put to bed, wanted Liz. She wanted a story, a drink, a cuddle, anything at all to reassure herself that Liz was there, that she too would not go out one fine day and never come back. If Liz went into the yard, or out of earshot, even for a moment, she was greeted on her return by a hysterical storm of tears which she did not know how to handle.

Often too Jane woke in the night, and Liz found herself exhausted by a screaming child who alternately clung to her and hit her, as if unable to resolve her own feelings at all. Sometimes Joe could quieten her, and sometimes Peter came in and stood wide-eyed and silent, and then crept back to his own bed and lay staring into the darkness.

On one of the worst of these nights the bull began lowing, and Liz carried Jane downstairs and out into the yard, anxious to find out what was wrong. Unusually, Casey was outside, prowling, unable to get to his companion because Joe had shut the half door. Jane watched quietly as Liz opened the door and let the cat inside, and grinned in spite of her tears when she saw Casey settle comfortably in the straw and start to wash the big beast.

'Sultan was lonely,' she said. 'I'm lonely in the night too.'

After that when she began to cry, Liz took her into her own bed. If the tears persisted they went to look at the bull, to check that Honey and Candy were sleeping, and to drink hot milk in the cosy kitchen with the Aga open and flames dancing on the wall. Slowly the nightmares grew less.

Paul Fenton had not left a will. His mother had no desire to leave her second husband or to have the children. She had deserted her first family many years before, and for the first time, when he read her letter, Joe realized what Jill's defections must have meant to her husband, whose mother had left his father when he was only ten, and whose wife appeared to be following in a similar path.

By the time winter came the Fenton house was sold, and strangers lived in it. The money was banked and put away for the children, and the village knew that as soon as the papers were through the children would be adopted by the Waymans.

'If we're your children don't we get called Wayman?' Peter asked one morning, pushing away his breakfast egg.

Joe looked at him, not at all sure of his ground.

'You could be ... or you needn't. Doesn't matter to anyone but you ... and us,' he said at last.

'Then I think we could be,' Peter said. 'It's not so muddly at school with the same name ... then we don't have to explain. I don't like explaining. And then when I grow up I can be Farmer Wayman too,' he added as an afterthought. 'I like being a farmer.'

And he'll make a good one, Joe thought, looking across the table at the boy, who was once more eating his egg, having disposed of what had apparently been a major problem. Peter was good with animals, interested in the day-to-day management of the beasts, eager to point out cuts on the cattle, and even ready to help dress an abscess the size of his fist that Cherry had acquired after injuring herself on barbed wire.

'I think it's time we gave proper riding lessons, like Nat says you're going to,' Jane said, her mouth so full that it was hard to hear her. 'I told the girls at school that we were going to, and there's Diana, and Mary and Susan Green and Susan Howarth and Samantha and Gloria all want to come. And Jeremy Carne, only I don't like him much. He pulls cats' tails.'

'Well!' Liz said, startled, and looked across to find Joe grinning at her.

'Railroaded,' he said. 'Sounds as if you'd better make a start ... only thing is, kids, it's a lot of work, and you'll have to help.'

'Super!' Jane said. She buttered her third slice of toast. 'I'll help. I'll tell them, "Heels down. Sit in the centre of your saddle. Don't pull on his mouth." '

'You'll do no such thing,' Liz said, laughing. 'That'll be my job. But you can help get the ponies ready, and the saddles cleaned. And help with the feeding. The ponies will need extra feed when they're working.'

'I do that already,' Peter said. 'And what's more, I looked in the book about horses yesterday and it says mares in foal need special rations and I don't think Honey's getting a proper diet!'

'And that was my sentiments, not yours, young feller-me-lad,' Mike Flynn said, coming into the room with a file of cats behind him. Tartar and Casey came first, eager to find their breakfast, and Midge followed, bringing all four kittens along, having decided it was time for them to be weaned. She was much too exhausted to catch mice for them. She mewed at Liz, who got up and began to look for four more saucers, and crumble bread into them to soak with milk.

'She is having extra feed,' Joe said, watching the cats line up and begin to eat with a noise that was quite incredible for such small animals. The kittens gulped louder than any of them, and made Jane and Peter grin at one another. The kids were settling down at last, he thought contentedly.

'I didn't see any,' Peter said.

'She's got her own bin, hadn't you noticed? Special mixture for foaling mares, young Mr. Know-All.'

'Thought your dad wouldn't make that sort of mistake,' Mike said incautiously.

'He's not my dad,' Peter was quick to deny the statement. He looked at Joe thoughtfully. 'But he's as good as.'

He went out to the stables to water the horses, and Liz caught Joe's eye. There was no need for words.

'Hear you're actually starting that riding school, at long

last,' Mike said, pausing in the doorway, before grooming Starlight. 'Want a riding master?'

'Who told you? And yes, I do.' Liz was suddenly eager to get started. It would be fun to have the place full of children, and to teach again. She loved teaching. And it would be good for Jane and Peter.

'Jane told me. Said it was all planned and you'd got some pupils.'

Liz laughed.

'Jane jumped the gun, but it's a good idea. I'm sending her out to tout for me. Won't need to advertise.'

Jane, her arms full of kittens, gave a small secret satisfied grin. It was going to be fun, and she would be able to tell all her friends just what to do. She was the one with the ponies. They hadn't got ponies. She went outside and put the kittens beside the haystack, where they attacked Casey, who bore with them good-humouredly, patting gently at any that was too fierce. Jane went to feed Candy, and stand beside her, and admire her foal, now grown and leggy and friendly, so long as no one tried to catch him. He would nuzzle a hand or rub against a shoulder, but he treasured his freedom, and ran off at once at any sign of greater familiarity. Mike had trained him to walk on a halter rope, but he did not like it.

When Liz looked out of the kitchen window as she prepared the potatoes for dinner she saw that Mike had taken all the saddles outside and was busy with saddle soap, Jane and Peter cross-legged on the ground rubbing at the bridles. They would need more saddles, and new girths, and in time more ponies to fill the field. She whipped up the children's milkshakes and made the coffee and whistled.

She was going to be very busy, but life was going to be much more fun.

CHAPTER FOURTEEN

By Easter time Liz had forgotten what it was like to be without children. Jane and Peter brought home their friends, who came to see the new piglets, the chicks, the calves, the dogs and the cats, and who proved to have homes ever ready to welcome a kitten or a puppy. There was never any difficulty in disposing of the litters.

Once they had visited the farm, the children returned. It was much more fun to play in the big barn, jumping from the hay loft into the straw, to race with the dogs and cats, to dangle inviting lengths of string for the kittens, to help feed the ponies and the pigs and the chickens, to watch Starlight in the big field, where Mike Flynn had rigged up a number of jumps, and to have their own lessons on the ponies, sometimes with Liz but more often with Mike, whose retirement seemed to have become busier than his working days. His wife did not mind. It kept him happy and nothing was worse than a discontented man under foot all day, brooding over past glories.

'We ought to run a village gymkhana,' Mike said one evening as he fed Honey. Her foal was almost due. She waited patiently for him to put hay in the rack. She was the gentlest of creatures, and Liz had a special feeling for the little mare, who in her turn adored Liz, and would follow her round the yard, and through the fields, dog-like, asking occasionaly for extra fuss and attention.

Mike's idea proved popular. Many of the village children were coming for riding lessons, especially as Liz had not the heart to charge very much. Her accountant made loud moaning noises because he was sure she would be out of pocket, but in fact the farm could stand the loss. Joe was good at making money with his animals, and had an eye for a beast, often buying cheaply and selling at a profit.

The older members of the village came too. The doctor's wife, Sara Lynton, started hacking every week. Her husband, Dave, came whenever he could find the time, took out Benty, a half-Irish hunter that Joe had bought in the Autumn Beast Sale. Benty was an amiable fool, loving to pretend terror of small creatures like frogs and birds, yet quite unafraid of tractors, bull-dozers, and double-decker buses, which put even Honey into a flurry of alarm.

The chef from the big hotel which had just opened at the entrance to the new motorway, the village dentist, the silent solicitor who had taken over the Fentons' house, and who never had more than a nod for anyone, and several people from Glassford, all helped to make Liz's week busy. It became necessary to plan the rides, ensuring that no pony or horse was overworked, or taken out twice running, and constant grooming and saddle cleaning began to occupy more and more of each day, particularly in wet weather.

It was fun to wake in the morning and open the stables and see the quiet beasts waiting, each head turning impatiently as light flooded in.

Jane and Peter were busy too. No room for passengers on a farm. Peter took over the chickens and brought water to the ponies. Jane took Honey and Candy under her own care, and staggered round the yard with the hay bales at night, spreading them thick for bedding. Peter helped Mike and Lew and Nat to muck out stables and byres and sties, and grew two inches and put on weight, and became tanned and sturdy and independent. Liz, watching the children, hoped that the bad days were forgotten. Jane slept soundly at night, and although needing to reassure herself, often, that both Liz and Joe were there, and would return from any trip they made, she had gained assurance, and was obviously content.

Easter came and went with a flurry of preparation, and a party for all the children in the big Church Hall. Liz, helping for the first time, found herself making new friends among the mothers of the children who came to her for riding lessons. Mike's wife, Nora, proved invaluable, with new ideas for sandwich fillings, and she was a dab hand at making paper hats and table decorations.

Before the party was over the gymkhana had become a fact, with a committee organized to plan it and the big field behind Wayman's Corner, which Mike used for Starlight, already agreed upon for the event.

Only one thing marred the passing days. The bull was becoming more and more irritable. At night, when Casey was with him, he was quiet, but during the day his noise became irksome, and several times he vented his rage on his pen, crashing his horn against the door, once shattering the framework, another time liffting the top corner off its hinges. Lew, mucking out one morning, the bull held in the yoke, saw the beast's head turn and the horn thrust towards him and jumped hastily backwards.

'Don' like the little 'uns,' Lew decided. 'Too noisy, by 'alf.'

He was becoming more talkative. Mainly because Jane spent most of her time at home following him around prattling and demanding answers. Lew was not used to people who wanted to hear his opinion. He enjoyed the new bustle on the farm, the constant coming and going of cars and people, he enjoyed seeing the rides go out, five or six ponies in file, and was always at the gate to welcome them in, grinning as he saw how the novice riders could not completely control mounts that were eager to reach their stables and food and familiar places, and broke into trot or canter as soon as they smelt home.

'Why don't you take the kids out with the Hunt?' Joe asked one morning, when frost greyed the grass and the air was sharp. 'They'd find it fun.'

'Might try.' Liz was short-tempered. Something had upset Sultan in the early hours and his constant low had become maddening. 'I wish Jane wouldn't entice Casey away from that beast. It's ridiculous but he's much quieter when the cat's with him.'

'Only a phase,' Joe said. 'He gets these brooding fits. He'll get over it. Hunt's meeting outside the Wheatsheaf on Saturday. If Nat'll come in and help out, I'll take Starlight, and Mike Flynn can have Benty. Jane can come on Candy.'

'Don't suppose Peter will come at all.' Liz was watching Jane walk round the yard pulling a string for Casey to chase. The bull called and the cat answered, off-hand, engrossed in his own affairs, unwilling to abandon the tempting dingle-dangle mouse-tail cord that was for ever just out of his reach. No cat could resist a string, and Jane knew that well. Soon Tartar joined them, but Jane tired of the game before the cats and left them pulling at the string between them.

Casey was agile again, hiding his limp with an odd sidle, and he could run as fast as the other cats. He was ratting again, and had laid waste a nest of baby weasels, luckily when their mother was out foraging. He had tangled with another fox, and left his antagonist with a badly scratched nose, while the cat had a bitten ear and a slow-healing abscess that irritated him more than it hurt.

Another three weeks, and Honey would foal. There would not be time to go hunting then. Need to be there in case anything went wrong.

By Saturday Jane was too excited to eat. Liz was riding Merry, a grey pony that Joe had bought from a farmer in the next county, an obliging and willing little beast. He and Candy were stable mates and best not separated. As long as one led the other would follow, and whenever they were put in the field together they were sure to be found side by side. If one was taken out without the other, long welcoming calls resounded across several fields as the pony left behind neighed eagerly, hating his loneliness.

The local Hunt was a very mixed affair, that the bigger Hunts would have scorned. Townsfolk, hiring a horse for the day, and glad to get any mount at all, no matter how they looked; farmers and their children, some on good-looking hunters, some on rangy cobby beasts with wild eyes and over-sensitive ears; children from local riding stables, on a motley collection of ponies.

Outside the Wheatsheaf was minor pandemonium. Hounds milled, the Huntsman calling them to order, old friends greeted one another, children rode too close to each other, and their ponies jostled and shied. Sue Burton's little grey mare Susie bit John Mills's Jackanory. Candy decided to dance in temper when Starlight backed towards her, annoyed in his turn by a bay mare who suddenly lashed out a hind leg.

At last they were off, trotting down the lane towards the wide spread of the green, along behind the new estate, on to the bridle path that was still usable though overgrown and nettle-edged, and over the hump-backed canal bridge to the first covert, where the hounds gave sudden tongue, and were off after a flash of rusty fur as the fox tore out of a coppice and flung himself along the ditch.

Liz, anxious to keep close to Jane, did not at first notice that they had other company. The hounds were well ahead, the field strung out, and she and Jane behind. She had no desire to be in at the death if there were a kill, but she loved the ride, the jumps over hedges and gates and small rippling brooks, and the excitement that bubbled and spilled all around her.

'Hey, look!' Jane yelled and pointed and burst into laughter.

Liz glanced behind her and gasped, for there, following as fast as they were able, were Tich and Casey. Casey, seeing her, gave a pleased yowl that made the pony in front shy so that his rider gave Liz a furious glare before galloping off to catch up with the rest of the field.

'We'll have to take them back,' Liz said. 'They might get lost . . . or trampled on.'

The fox had doubled on his tracks. Desperate, never hunted before, and terrified by the noise, the thud and thunder of hooves, the baying hounds, the panting mouths that came red and close, the Huntsman's yells of encouragement, the sounding horn, he had lost his head completely. Panic-mad, he jumped the massed backs of the pack, that milled on itself, witless, unable to turn or move in the narrow lane in which it was caught. Liz and Jane watched as the Huntsman tried to sort the tangle, as the horses turned, and the fox fled between their legs, all the riders now in front of the hounds.

Casey hissed and spat and leaped on to Jane's saddle, and Tich, unable to restrain himself, broke into noisy excited barking that drove the fox frantic, pell-mell, into a sheepfield. Here he took cover in the milling flock.

Harried by the dog, driven wild by their own fear, the sheep packed closer and closer and the fox lay in their midst until, seeing an opening, he fled again through them, through a hole in the wall, along the canal bank, under the bridge, and into the drain of a half-flooded culvert where he swam to the end, and emerged, slime covered, shivering, a sorry-looking object, to taste the air, and find that he was now alone. Liz and Jane had seen him, but they looked at one another and said nothing.

Five minutes later the Hunt came to Wayman's Corner, where Lew, his check cap askew, his round face a-grin, had seen the fox dive safe to earth in what he knew was a very deep drain that went underground and came out again in the top field. He took a shovelful of stable dung and smeared it at the entrance to the drain. When the Hunt came by he looked at them innocently, the spade hidden in the long grass, mouth meeker than thistledown.

'Owd fox, went thataway,' he said, pointing towards the church, and pushed his cap further back on his head.

The Hunt turned again, horses milling in the lane, hooves clattering, tongues chattering, hounds muddling, twisting, eyes flashing as they sped, stern high, returning on the scent, spilling in a turmoil past Witchet's Corner, flying over Turton Brook, leaping on, thrusting and pushing, finding an errant trace of scent lying on the Bounty meadow, hurdling the fence at Sentry Farm, speeding towards the rust coloured dead-brackened slope.

Lew scratched his head and his grin broadened. There'd be no kill today. He'd foiled the Hunt, proper he had. And owd fox could run free again and father his fubsy cubs and reach March madness and run moon-crazed when the hares ran, and skitter hobgoblin wild in the shimmering May meadows.

The fox, lurking crouched in a slime-speckled drain, heard the thudding hooves die away to a mutter and then pass out of earshot. The ground no longer shook beneath the tramp and tread. He flicked his ears and crept out. Lew saw him crouch at the edge of the ditch, his nose asking the wind what danger lay on his twisting homeward way.

Nothing troubled the air. He slipped away and Lew grinned again, proud to be cleverer than all the hunting folk, for all their better schooling and wisdom and knowledge. He, with only a few of the wits that God gave to most men, knew, better than any of them, the tricks owd fox played, and owd hare too, and what was more he could gentle a beast that even Vet couldn't handle. Like Sultan there.

Lew listened uneasily. Sultan was uncommon cranky these days, worse than he'd ever been, and it took more time to soothe him. Seemed as if there was summat wrong wi' beast. An abscess growing deep inside him, mebbe, or a wild ache from an illness that no one could see. Tricky tempered all the time, was owd bull these days.

Tich came running home, annoyed because he'd lost his fox. He jumped up at Lew and Lew knelt and laid his face against the dog's face. The terrier licked him, between the two of them a perfection of understanding.

Jane, trotting back with Casey balanced on the saddle, her hand holding him firm, saw them and waved, and Lew came and took the cat and held the purring little beast closely, deriving more pleasure from the act than from anything else he knew. Girls terrified Lew. He hated being touched by anyone, recoiling like an animal from man or woman, not allowing even Nat to put a hand on his shoulder, but contact with beasts soothed him. You could trust an animal. Dislike you and an animal bit you, or if it was a cow or horse, might kick you. If it liked you you always knew. Not like people, who smiled to your face and were bitter cruel behind your back.

He unsaddled the horses.

Jane and Liz dropped into the chairs in the kitchen, aching from their ride, enjoying a companionable silence. Time enough to get up and do when Joe came home.

Peter, whistling through the door, looked at his sister.

'Did you like your hunting?' he asked.

'No,' said Jane. 'It's nicer riding quietly, just me and you and Mike and Liz and Joe. Too many horses are frightening.'

'Girls are cissies,' Peter said, ignoring the fact that he had not even wanted to go. He slapped his hazel switch against his shoe and whistled between his teeth like Lew, and swaggered out of the room.

'That boy's getting impossible,' Jane said.

Liz laughed, and began to make the tea.

CHAPTER FIFTEEN

THE cattle were waiting for Ken Lewis to test them for tuberculosis. It was a familiar chore, though not familiar to the cows who were bewildered because they were penned behind the milking parlour instead of being taken back to roam free in the meadow. It was easier for Ken to manage them in the milking stalls, where they were unable to move or back away, though those that hated the process could still toss an angry head, and stamp.

The lowing cattle disturbed the bull. He hated change, hated breaks in his routine, hated the noisy children who ran round the yard, and who, in spite of Liz's remonstrances and Mike's chiding, often forgot that they had to be quiet in the presence of big animals, who were often much more nervous than small ones.

'A horse sees two pictures,' Mike often told them. 'One with one eye and one with the other. He has to think and decide which picture matters ... which one is perhaps dangerous ... the car coming towards him on his left, or you racing after him on his right. And he can't bear people who come up quietly from behind him. You *must* tell him you are there. Call out ... "hey Benty", and he'll turn his head and see you and know you're around. How'd you like it if I crept up behind you and suddenly slapped you on the back?'

This particular morning the worst of all the children was coming for a ride. It was unfortunate that it should coincide with the Vet's visit.

Roger Leigh was the spoilt and only son of the owner of a big manufacturing business. What Roger wanted, he was used to getting. Just now he wanted to ride, and then have his own pony, and then go in for Show jumping, and he had already entered for the gymkhana, which was almost completely organized. All that was needed was the final preparation and a fine day.

Unfortunately, Roger was rude, and noisy, and infuriated Liz in a shorter time than any child she had ever known. He was almost eleven, big for his age, with clumsy hands that tugged at the pony's mouth, and a vicious temper if his mount refused to obey, which, as Roger was slow to learn, and unwilling to change his ways, was often. Liz never knew whether to give him an obedient pony and risk having its temper spoiled, or one of the more stubborn animals, who might get mistreated, but would not react so adversely as little Candy or tiny gentle Toss or the other fell pony, Pitch, who was always edgy and who became unreasonably alarmed whenever the bull bellowed.

Today Sultan was venting his wrath, lowing continuously, pawing the straw, rubbing one horn irritably against the framework of the door, his eyes glaring at everyone who passed by the pen.

'Goin' to be a bad day. Owd bull won't even listen,' Lew said forlornly. 'Think he's mebbe sick.'

'Think he's mebbe black bad tempered, rotten owd beast,' Nat said morosely. He had torn his finger on barbed wire, rescuing one of the next-door sheep that had escaped and managed to half immerse itself in a cattle trough that had been abandoned under a fence in the hay field. Going to clean trough up one day and put it into far meadow to make another watering place for cattle . . . somehow one day never came. Too much to do, Nat thought, his finger throbbing. Have to take it to doctor, gone septic stupid owd thing, only a little tear. And bull to muck out, and him getting nowtier than ever. Goin' to be a bad day, Nat grumbled to himself, as he led Scotty out and saddled him. Scotty was a new pony, only bought last week. Scotty'd show that beastly lil Roger Leigh what was what. Most awkward of all the ponies, but Mis' Liz hadn't realized it.

Scotty submitted to saddling and bridling. He was edgy too, hating the bull's noise, and nervous of the dogs. He had been bitten by a dog in his foal days, and never liked them since. Tich, roaming too near, was just missed by a lashing hoof.

Had Mike been there that day, Scotty would have remained in his stable. Mike had noticed an unevenness in the pony's gait, and had meant to ask Joe to have the Vet look him over when he came to test the cattle. But Nora Flynn had poured a kettle full of boiling water over her hand, and was out of action, and Mike was at home, coping with the household affairs, while his wife fretted, sure he was doing everything wrong.

Liz looked in at Honey. Ken must look at her too. Only a week or so before the foal was due, and foals, like babies, often decided to come early. No leaving a mare to foal alone. And Honey was especially nervous. She'd need watching, every minute of the birth, and soothing and gentling.

The mare greeted her listlessly. She was uncomfortable and bothered, and it was not easy for her to move. It was going to be a very big foal. Liz was worried. She had rung Honey's previous owners and they had had no idea that there was to be a foal, but remembered a stray stallion a couple of months or so before she was sold. Perhaps he had been in the field. He was a big grey. And Honey was tiny. How could people be so careless, Liz wondered, and barely glanced at Roger, who had come into the yard, flourishing his birthday present, a new horsewhip with a dog's head silver handle.

Bennie backed away from the slashing whip and snarled. He hated Roger, who did not look where he was going and often trod on the dogs' paws. Tich, seeing him coming, had hastily absented himself on pressing business elsewhere and Casey had gone with him. The whip flashed again, this time within a few feet of the bull's head, and Sultan roared in outrage.

'Do be careful, Roger,' Liz said. 'Are you ready?'

Roger mounted Scotty, who stood deceptively still. He was pondering two possible moves; he could either go to the bucket beneath the tap and demand a drink, which would delay everything for a considerable time, or he could duck his head into Honey's stable and steal some pony nuts from the bag near the door. Either possibility was delectable and guaranteed to put off the evil moment when he would have to trot out on to the wide drive, and into the narrow lane, where anything might happen. Puffing monsters snorted towards him, as the tractors passed on their way to the farms; giant red roaring contraptions full of people hurtled down the road, and sometimes bayed their horns at him, little buzzing cars and big whining cars harried him, making him long for the sanctuary of the quiet field and peace of the stable.

Nat, glowering, his head aching, opened the door of the bull-pen and dodged the horned head and fastened the neck yoke that held the beast more or less immovable

172

while the soiled straw was forked out. He gave the bull some hay, but Sultan was too unsettled to feed. Everything about him was noisy today, and nobody talked soothingly to him, and Lew was busy elsewhere and Casey had left him. His moans continued, growing louder every time he opened his mouth.

'Oh, give over, yer gurt bastard,' Nat muttered furiously.

Scotty made up his mind. Roger, who had not been concentrating, was startled as the pony walked swiftly to the bucket, and put his head inside. There was very little water, and Scotty rattled the pail noisily against the brick wall.

'Stupid beast,' Roger said furiously and lashed the pony's shoulders with the whip.

There was a sore place at the top of the right foreleg, that was causing the lameness that Mike had noticed. The flicked whip caught the bruise and Scotty reared, his flailing forehooves thundering against the drainpipe. The noise horrified him. He came down, his left fore catching the bucket with a resounding din that made him think there were devils after him. Nat came running. Liz grabbed for the reins, but the pony had had enough. He hurtled into the centre of the yard and bucked violently, sending Roger flying over his head to land with an appalling thump on the cobbles.

Liz handed Merry to Nat and ran to the boy. He was bruised and shaken and furious, and standing up, began to yell at Liz.

'He's a hateful pony. I hate your stupid stables. You haven't got a decent horse here.'

Liz left him in disgust.

Scotty was berserk, and it was impossible to get near him. The sound of iron shoes on metal had driven him crazy, the bruise on his shoulder had flared to agony after the cut with the whip, the bellowing bull offended his ears, the clatter of his own hooves on cobbles added to his fear. He continued to buck and kick out at anyone who came near him.

'Get in car, yer damned lil booger, and shut oop, will yer?' Nat shouted, too angry to care what anyone thought of him. Roger, who had never been spoken to in such a way in his life, gave the man an astounded stare and climbed into Liz's car, thoroughly upset by the sight of the enraged pony, and sure that someone would be hurt before long. So long as it wasn't him. . . .

Lew heard the pandemonium and came running. He was out of breath, and it was some minutes before he recovered his voice. Ken Lewis was just in time to see the angry pony calm slowly as Lew's soft tones coaxed and soothed and wheedled. Ken took a handful of pony nuts and Scotty accepted the peace offering, and allowed Lew to lead him into the dark stable.

Ken noticed the limp.

'Dry him down and I'll have a look at him when I've done the cattle,' he said.

Nobody had been watching the bull. Nat, turning to finish mucking out, found himself face to face with a mountain of fury. The noise had so terrified the beast that he had burst the yoke and now stood, head lowered, swaying his horns from side to side.

'My God!' Ken said. 'Get a couple of hayforks, Nat, quickly, man.'

Nat turned to go, and slipped. His foot caught the bull on the foreleg, and the massive animal charged, unaware of anything except that now he was free and could have his way with the men who kept him penned, forgetting that they fed him and coaxed him and gentled him, only aware of rage that made him want to harm everything that was in his way.

Terror lent Nat more wits than he knew he had and he rolled away from the bull, who overran him, and turned, head lowered, shaking it from side to side as he tried to find his enemy. Nat rolled under the horse trough and lay still. No good trying to stand. At least he was safe here. The thing was stone and just enough space underneath for him to fit. Please God owd bull didn't charge Vet.

Joe, who had been in the milking parlour, coping with Cherry who was also in a bad mood, came running just in time to see Ken dodge over the fence, falling heavily to the ground, and Liz bolt for the kitchen. The boy in the car had crouched down on the floor, scared stupid by the bull. There was nowhere for Joe to go. The beast saw him and thundered towards him, and Joe leaped sideways and then leaped again, as a sweeping horn caught the shoulder of his coat and tore it with a rending sound that maddened the animal even more.

Lew, looking out of the stable, gasped in horror. There was only one thing to be done and he wasn't sure if he had time. The bull was charging again. Joe was caught between the walls of the stables, that were set at an angle to one another, but he was too far away from any of the open doors. He could dodge for a bit longer, but in a few minutes he would tire, or fall, and then . . .

Lew swung himself into the loft above Scotty's stable. It was a huge place continuing above all the stalls. At the end was an old door that led out into the open air. It hadn't been opened for years and there was no way down. There was not time to think. Luckily it was not too stiff. It opened, and Lew lowered himself from the sill, holding on with his hands, and then dropped to the ground and ran as he had never run before, going in front of the house, climbing through the dining-room window and racing into the kitchen.

His hands were steady as he grabbed the gun and loaded it. Liz watched him, her face white. She could do nothing but look from the window as Joe ducked and dodged and Ken tried to distract the bull by waving his coat. Neither of them stood a chance.

Lew came out of the door and yelled, waving his hands and the gun above his head. Sultan heard him, turned towards him, and goaded beyond endurance, thudded across the yard. Lew sighted. The gun spoke. Once. Twice. Lew jumped clear, and slowly, incredibly, the great beast fell, his blood reddening the cobbles. Lew dropped the gun. He could not see for the tears streaming down his face. He knelt beside the bull.

'Owd bull,' he said. 'Owd bull.'

His hands caressed the wrinkled neck, gentled the soft head, and moved towards the slowly glazing eyes. There was nothing more to do. Owd bull was gone, no longer magnificent. Lew's tears would not stop, and they flowed all the faster when Casey came into the yard, and curious, walked towards the pair of them and sniffed at the bull.

And sat down and keened to the sky above him, a desolate wail that made the dogs howl and the cattle low, until all the farmyard animals seemed to be mourning the passing of their king.

CHAPTER SIXTEEN

LIZ was used to chaos, but not chaos like this. Ken was standing with his back against the stable wall, his eyes closed and his face white, as he nursed his right arm with his left hand, and Liz saw, with horror, that the hand was swollen and purple, at an odd angle at the wrist. Blood was pouring down Joe's coat, both hands were bleeding, and his face was scraped along one side, where he had hit his head against the rough corner of the stable wall.

Useless to try and do anything with Lew. She left him there, beside the dead bull, while Casey's eerie noise tore at her so that she had a lump in her throat and a sick feeling in her stomach, and a raw taste in her mouth. She glanced at her watch. The children were due home from the errand on which she had, luckily, sent them, and, as if catching her thought, they came laughing, through the big white barred gate, and then stopped, staring, appalled, and ran to her.

'The bull went crazy,' Liz said.

Peter was used to emergencies. There was nothing for him to do here, but he could help.

'I'll ring for the doctor,' he said, his eyes questioning. Liz nodded.

'And, Peter, cancel the rest of today's rides. Tell them

we've had an accident with the cattle. I don't know . . .'

Peter had already gone. A year of farm life had already taught him that animals often caused emergencies. He knew that he had to cope. He rang the doctor first and then sat down with the diary of rides, tracing each name patiently on Liz's small directory pad, which listed all the telephone numbers she needed. Rides often had to be changed as a horse might go lame, or be off-colour, or some farm matter of more urgency might intervene. Luckily people were understanding.

Except for Roger's people, Liz, thought in horror, as Roger's mother turned her E-type Jaguar in through the gate and stopped with a showy screech of tyres that made Starlight kick his hind hooves furiously against the back of his stall. He hated the noise that the Leigh car always made. And there was no telling the silly bitch, either, Liz thought angrily as she schooled her lips to a smile and started to apologize for the cancellation of Roger's ride.

She had no chance. The boy exploded from her car, grabbing his mother, shrieking his terror. It made the dogs bark, set the cattle lowing and set Casey off again on his eerie wail, so that Jane grabbed him and held him with tears pouring down her cheeks, and Starlight kicked and kicked again and Honey neighed in utter panic and Scotty, who had been quiet, pawed the straw angrily and neighed shrilly too.

'For Christ's sake shut lil stoopid booger oop,' Nat shouted through the din.

He had put out a hand to quieten Starlight and been nipped for his trouble. The stallion rarely bit, but the noise was more than he could bear and he had no other way of soothing his outraged feelings. Ken had gone in to look at Honey, stumbling as he walked. Joe was with

Scotty. Lew might have been in a trance. The blood from the bull oozed slowly on to the cobbles.

'How dare he speak to me like that!' Mrs. Leigh was a small woman, red-haired, her thin bitter mouth a slash of scarlet in a face that was white with temper. Few people ever dared cross her. She was notorious for having changed all her tradespeople more often than anyone else in the village and the manageress of the dress shop in Glassford quailed when she saw her coming.

'Do more than speak.' Nat was angrier than he had ever been in his life, was aware that Liz was shaking with reaction and quite unable to deal with the situation, was anxious about Lew who sat like a dumb thing as if his few wits had gone for ever, was wanting to get Jane out of the way, and intent on making this idiot go and take her squalling brat with her.

He lifted the hay fork which had been his main weapon when the bull charged.

'Stoof this up yer arse if yer don't get out.'

'Nat!' Liz expostulated, and then hysteria overtook her, and she began to laugh helplessly, knowing that in a moment her laughter would turn to sobbing and that she could not control one or the other, or cope with the situation at all.

'You'll hear more of this!' Janet Leigh had never been so treated in her life. She demanded the deference that was only due to her because her husband had more money than most people, and usually she received it, although, from Liz, it was only the politeness that she extended to everyone, rich or poor alike.

Liz gasped, and almost choked. Jane had crept to her side, and was leaning against her. She must control herself for the child's sake. She stopped laughing, suddenly furious.

'Get out! Can't you see you're in the way, that we've got things to do, that people are hurt? Get out, and don't you ever bring that beastly child back. If it hadn't been for him and his damned whip none of this would have happened.'

'I want my whip,' Roger yelled.

Liz saw it lying on the cobbles. She picked it up, and broke it over her knee.

'I'll sue you for that!' Janet Leigh could scarcely mouth the words.

'Try it.' Joe had come out of the stable, his face thunder-dark. 'And we'll sue you . . . that boy has caused the death of a bull that was worth nearly a thousand pounds, he's caused injury to two horses, and to me, and to Nat, and he's caused Mr. Lewis, the Vet, to break his arm. If you want to sue us, try it. See where it gets you.'

'And you can take that spoilt over-sexed poodle of yours to someone else,' Ken added, the pain from his arm making him incautious. 'Now get out!'

Peter closed the gate behind the car, and came back to Liz, who was trembling so much that she had to sit down on the edge of the horse trough. She wiped Jane's eyes, and stroked Casey, who was still wailing in a soft uncanny voice.

'Liz!' Peter's voice was urgent.

Liz turned to him, hoping he was not going to ask some awkward question.

'Jane and me can look after Mrs. Mike. Would you like Mike?'

'He'd be a godsend,' Liz said. 'But can you look after his wife? She can't use her hand at all.'

'She can tell us what to do,' Jane said, glad of anything that would get her away from the farmyard. She could not look at the dead bull without shuddering convulsively. Lew's immobility terrified her, and Casey made her cry. 'We only have to do what she says.' She was eager to go right away and not return until her world was normal again. Liz bent her head and kissed her, guessing the child's thoughts.

'Send Mike quickly,' she said.

Ken put his head out of Honey's stable.

'Tell him Honey's foaling . . . and she's hurt,' he said.

'Ken!' Liz took Casey from Jane, and set him on the ground. He walked back to the bull, rubbed his head against the stiff carcase, and wailed again.

'Oh, Casey!' Liz picked the cat up and shut him in the small stable reserved for the dogs. Here he continued to wail, even more upset because he was alone, and locked in, and in the dark. His yowls became deafening.

'Oh!' Liz said, pushing her hair back out of her eyes. It was too tame an exclamation. She glanced round quickly. Joe had gone into Honey's stable, Nat was standing beside Lew, trying to coax him to leave the bull and come and help. The children were already small figures in the distance, running fast. She went in to see Honey, who had knocked her head against a rafter as she reared, and had cut the skin.

The mare was lying down, her body twisted. Again and again she tried to stand, tossing her head, showing the whites of terrified eyes, looking desperately up at Liz, begging for comfort. Liz dropped on to her knees, cradling the injured head, smoothing the soft cheek, murmuring gently.

'It's all right, Honey. It's all right, girl.'

It was far from all right. The mare was in torment, her coat dark with sweat, every muscle straining. Ken, dizzy with pain, had managed to examine her, to feel the foal, to discover that not only was it very large, but that one leg was curled beneath its head. It required manipulation, and here was he, dear God, as helpless as a baby, with his arm useless. He'd have to try and tell Joe ... but it wasn't going to be easy and ten to one they'd kill the mare between them. The stable wall reeled towards him and he sat down abruptly in the straw.

'Will she be all right?'

Liz's voice brought him slowly back to reality. He put his head between his knees. Everything seemed a very long way off.

'God alone knows!' he said weakly, and it was no comfort at all.

Joe had gone to open the gate. Liz heard the sound of wheels in the yard as a car stopped gently. The door slammed and she heard the welcome sound of the local doctor's voice. Dave Lyndon was one of their regular riders, a clever man with a horse, and an understanding way with him. His wife, Sara, also a doctor, came riding too.

'Mercy on us.' He had a brisk cheerful voice, and he infused reality back into a scene that had long ceased to have any. 'Come on Lew, lad. Work to do.'

But not even Dave Lyndon could shake Lew back into the world. His own had ceased when he shot the bull and he could not forget that it was his hand that dealt the death wound. He should have calmed owd bull. Not as if her were that bad.

Dave left him, looked at Joe and whistled.

'Ken's worse off than me.'

Ken was lying back against the wall, wondering if he was going to die first or just be sick. He was not at all sure.

'Ambulance and hospital for you,' Dave said, bending over him.

Ken leaped back to life.

'Not bloody likely. The mare's foaling and there isn't another vet for miles. I'll have to stay. She's in a bad way. Patch me up, and give me something to tide me over. Then mebbe Joe can ring my mother and tell her to find a locum, quick, and you can put me wherever you like when that foal's safe.'

'And when will that be?' Dave asked, busy with his syringe.

'Call yourself a doctor, and ask that.' Ken's voice was scathing, but Dave merely grinned. The Vet wouldn't pass out on him now.

Nat came and stood looking at them, his face glum, his cap pushed back at an angle to his head. He had a nasty little bite to add to the septic place on his hand and his head was going to burst.

'Scotty's lamer than ever. Think her dragged a muscle plunging an' rearing when that damned little booger were 'ere,' he said, not to anyone in particular. 'And Starlight's bruised right foreleg. And I wish to 'eaven that bloody lil owd cat'd shut oop.'

'For goodness' sake, Nat,' Liz said irritably. 'Mind your language and in future don't talk like that to people who come here for rides. It won't do.'

'Wouldn't do it to no one else,' Nat said irritably. 'It deserved t'owd cow.'

He shambled off. Dave Lyndon caught sight of the filthy bit of rag he had put on his hand.

'Nat!' The doctor's voice was sharp. 'Go and get those hands of yours clean . . . and I mean clean, and then let me see what you're hiding under that unsavoury looking bandage.'

Nat stamped off, and glared at Mike who had come on a neighbour's bicycle, and was puffing, breathless, leaning on the gate to get his wind back.

'Thank goodness you've come,' Liz said. 'I'll go and make coffee. We could all do with a drink.'

'Called the knacker yet?' Mike asked. 'Lew won't come to his senses till you have. Worshipped that beast . . . wrong side of idolatry, I reckon.'

Liz called the knacker, who promised to come within the hour. She made coffee and sandwiches, blotting out thought, conscious of Casey yowling in the stable, and of the stamp and rustle from Honey's stable. The little mare neighed frequently, an anguished protest that made the cattle low, and the dogs bark and whine sympathy. The farmer on the opposite side of the road was cutting hay; the tractor sounded a constant accompaniment to the din. The farm had never been so noisy, not even when the bull was restless, storming and tossing in his pen. It seemed impossible that he was dead. Soon she would realize it and be glad, but just now she was numb with exhaustion.

Dave Lyndon stretched his long legs in the biggest armchair and looked at her seriously.

'You're all in,' he said.

Liz nodded, and then grinned ruefully. 'It's been quite a day. The children haven't even had any dinner.'

'Nora will see to that.' Mike's big bulk was reassuring. 'Dr. Lyndon, Ken wants to know if you could do a Caesarian on the mare if he told you how? I can't get that foal's leg straight. It seems to be doubled back in a very odd way. I'll break it if I put a rope on, and there's no manipulating the foal. He's much too big for her.'

Dave Lyndon stared at Mike.

'You must be joking,' he said at last.

'Wish I was. But there isn't a vet for miles and none of them's a horse vet. Ken reckons you'll do as well as any of them. Says you used to do quite a lot of operating.'

'Man alive! That was years ago. Before I bought a country practice and started rusticating. Only spots and colds and the screws now ... Petley Green's a healthy place.'

'It's something you don't forget. And you get lots of practice with tractor accidents and road accidents and the farm men are always needing stitching up.' Mike was insistent. 'It's our only chance. Without it, mare's a goner.'

'How long can she wait? I've a thing or two to see to at home, and I must get Sara to take surgery for me and do one or two other little jobs. Can she wait an hour?'

'Not much longer,' Mike said, but Dave Lyndon was already gone, driving swiftly out into the road. Liz took sandwiches and went into the stable.

'Wish we could get Lew to come,' Ken said. He shook his head when Liz offered him food, but drank the coffee eagerly. His hand was splinted and bandaged and he had had an injection to ease the pain, but not as strong as the doctor had wished. He needed a clear head.

Liz knelt.

'Honey! Good girl, clever Honey,' she murmured, but the mare was beyond words, in a world of pain and endurance of her own, a bewildering terrifying world that she did not understand, for she had never foaled before.

'Lew's what they call a "whisperer" among horse men,' Ken said. He was talking for his own benefit, afraid of drifting back into his haze of discomfort.

The mare arched her neck, and tried to rise. Her legs disobeyed her brain and she neighed again.

'Need somewhere clean as possible for Dave to operate,' Ken said, trying to remember everything.

'We'll scald out the bull's pen. Get Nat. It won't take a minute,' Joe said, not even listening to his words or aware that they were nonsense. It would take at least an hour. He was mentally preparing his tools. Scalding water. And disinfectant. Brushes. Luckily he could bring in the giant heaters and blow it dry fast. Thank God for electricity.

Nat, feeling better for a hot drink and food and two aspirins, his hand clean and bandaged comfortably, was in a better mood. He began to remove the straw from the bull's pen, working willingly and quickly, as anxious as anyone else to help the mare.

'What's a whisperer?' Liz asked. If they kept talking the mare listened, her ears moving, as if the voices were reassurance.

'A man with a way with animals. There aren't many.' Ken held out his mug for more coffee. Liz filled it, adding extra sugar to combat the shock which she was sure Ken must be suffering. His colour was better, but he was in such obvious pain that she felt she ought to send him packing and never mind the mare.

Honey's pain had eased temporarily. Her anxious eyes followed every movement that Liz made, and she obviously felt happier when her mistress settled once more beside her and began to rub the sweat from her coat with a handful of straw.

'Lew's one of them . . . some sort of magnetism . . . or chemistry . . . I don't know. They can charm any beast. . . . One man I used to know, a devil with people, yet beasts in the Zoo would come to the bars when he called, and answer him, and the tigers purred at him and rubbed their heads and rolled like the great cats they are . . .'

The mare was back in her agony. Liz murmured to her, but she did not hear. Her body was racked by violent muscular contortions, as she strove to bring to birth the foal that could not be born. Liz remembered her own birth pains with sudden vividness, remembered lying alone in terrified agony, the hospital nurses too young and inexperienced to realize the terror that lies in solitude and pain and the instinctive fear of the unknown . . . and even of the known. No creature should be left to endure pain in solitude, Liz thought, and heard Casey lift his voice again in an appalling yowl.

'He'd better have a tranquillizing injection, poor little brute,' Ken said. He had often been amused by the communion between the cat and the bull. It was now far from funny.

The mare whinnied as Liz stood up, a protest that first made her hesitate and then go out determinedly and shake Lew, shake him until he lifted his head and stared at her.

'Lew. Honey's foaling. She's going to die unless we help her . . . do you understand . . . she's going to die. Listen!'

Honey had struggled to her feet, bringing Ken to his. She was pawing the straw. She whinnied, on a high note of terror that brought Lew back to the world again, so that he stared at Liz, appalled, and then ran. His hands touched the mare and she stood quiet, submissive, as he smoothed the tormented muscles, gentled her, murmuring to her.

'Lew. Can you stay with her for a while? Don't leave her for a moment? I want to make a phone call.' Ken walked towards the door.

Lew nodded.

He could never leave a beast in pain. He took straw

and began to rub her down, feeling her hide sleek and wet under his hands, dark with the sweat that poured off her.

Honey rubbed her head against him, pushing hard at his chest, as if the contact brought her ease. Her muzzle dropped into his hand, and he began to talk to her, saying anything that came into his head, his voice a lulling anodyne bringing temporary relief. Ken looked in again. There was nothing he could do for the moment and Honey was in safe hands. He went to look at Scotty, and found Mike poulticing the injury. Joe was busy with Starlight, who had not been fed with his usual midday ration and was furious, and Nat was busy with the cattle, putting straw into the racks in the milking stalls. They had been penned in the yard all day and were also hungry and were lowing in urgent protest. And it was milking time.

The bull-pen was scoured and clean and drying out. Dave would be back soon. Good job his wife was a doctor too, Ken thought. Some time he must marry Sue, and also get a partner. Never had an emergency like this before. He dropped wearily into the big armchair and rested his head against the embroidered cushion, his eyes closed. What a day!

Liz was busy mixing gruel for the mare. She might take it after the operation. And there would be no time later. Joe's shoulder was painful and it was obvious that she would have to help with the milking and see to the horses. Mike was going to be busy assisting Dave. Lew . . . she shrugged. No use relying on Lew. Her mind went back to the day Mike came with his whippet bitch – nearly two years ago. And now, another Caesarian – and much more tricky.

She fetched Casey from the stable. He curled into her

arms, head beneath her armpit, as if to shut out the world. His small body was rigid and unyielding and he had no purr for her when she stroked him. Ken showed her what he needed and managed to fill the syringe, and she held the cat for him as he injected the tranquillizer.

He yowled in soft protest as the needle sank in. Liz took him upstairs and put him on Jane's old jersey on Jane's bed. It might console him. He often slept on it during the day if the weather was bad. She watched the cat curl himself up and tuck his nose under his paws, obviously sleepy, and left him, feeling that this was one problem that was temporarily shelved.

She made fresh coffee. This time Ken drank his black. He would need a clear head. He had telephoned his mother who had assured him that she was doing her best to find a locum, and that she had been given three names. The first was unavailable, and she was about to ring the other two. But no one could come in time to operate on the mare.

'You were talking about whisperers,' Liz said, hoping to distract the Vet, and help him forget his own discomfort.

'The racing stables nearly always have one.' Ken sipped the scalding black liquid and burnt his tongue. 'It's funny . . . gypsies often have the knack, and Lew has it. More often than not it's someone quite illiterate . . . they tend to be animal themselves. In a way, I suppose, nervous, sensitive, able to understand the instinctive fears that bedevil the beasts. Able to quiet them with their voices, usually murmuring, soothing. Few people realize the power a gentle human voice has in reassuring a frightened animal. I make a lot of my clients grin because I talk to their dogs and cats, but that acts almost as well as a tranquillizer. You should know . . . you do it yourself instinctively.'

Liz did know, although she had not realized how often she used her voice to coax a sick beast to eat, or calm a cow when Joe was giving it a drench, or stand with Lew and talk when a cow was calving, knowing that in some way voices were reassuring.

'Seen men tame hawks like that ... and once knew a man who had only to say "hi" and any cat in the vicinity followed him, rubbing against his legs and rolling at his feet and purring fit to burst.'

Liz went to the window.

'Dave's back,' she said.

Ken nodded, and grinned to comfort her. He went out into the farmyard, where the sun was already throwing elongated shadows, and the swallows were skimming low after flies. He had never felt so unhappy in his life.

Liz followed him.

'Liz,' he said, turning to her, wanting to be fair, yet angry with himself for destroying her hope, possibly unnecessarily, 'you realize, don't you, that this has only the faintest chance of success? I've got to remember every step, instead of doing it myself ... there are things you don't even need to think about when you're doing the job on your own ... and Dave hasn't operated for years, and never on a horse.'

Liz put out her hand and touched Ken's cheek lightly.

'Don't worry, Ken,' she said. 'It's just one of those things.'

He nodded, went over to Dave and promptly forgot her, and she went to talk to the mare and watch her pawing and turning, and twisting, trying to free herself from the burden that was betraying her.

CHAPTER SEVENTEEN

THE knacker took away the bull. Nat scrubbed the blood from the cobbles. Milking was done and the cattle once more at peace in the field. The dogs lay, nose on paws, watching Nat and Lew and Liz as they worked. Joe busied himself with Liz's jobs, his arm held in a sling to ease the pain from his shoulder. The bull's horn had penetrated farther than he had realized.

The chickens were fed and locked in for the night, the horses and ponies quieted and stabled, once more placid, munching hay, the bedding thick beneath them. The shadows had lengthened and gone, the sun was only a memory, the lambent lampglow spilled through the kitchen door. Casey woke and came to Liz and curled on her knee, forlorn, refusing to eat. He lapped, just to oblige her, at a tin of condensed milk that she opened especially for him, knowing it was his delight, his downfall, that he loved to steal. Midge and Tartar finished it between them.

'They can't still be operating,' Liz said unhappily, toying with a Cornish pasty that she had made the day before. Lew had gone home, and come back again and was outside the door, watching the clouds slide over the moon and away again, playing an endless game of peep and go. An owl hooted long and lone from the big barn.

Nessie whined and quieted again. The clock struck yet another quarter. Joe did not even bother to reply. He was too exhausted to think of words to say. He traced the patterned line round the edge of his saucer with his finger, round and round, until Liz could have screamed.

Lew came into the kitchen and sat down on the windowsill, and Nat came in from the milking parlour, which he had been scrubbing out. Everything was done, at long last, and the chaos reduced to order. The cows would have to be tested another day.

Nat washed his hands, and came to Liz to have his bandages renewed.

'Reckon I shouldn't 'a said what I said.' Nat could never bear to apologize. 'Only that female riled me proper.'

'You shouldn't, Nat,' Liz agreed. She relented and smiled at him. 'None of us behaved very well, I suppose.'

'Proper rotten owd day. Yer coming home, our Lew?'

'Wanna see Honey's foal,' Lew said. He had been drinking tea, but his appetite was gone. The bull-pen was silent, in spite of the men inside it and the mare and the foal coming. How could it all be so quiet? And how was it that, although the bull was dead, his memory still brooded over the farmyard, so that at any moment they all expected to hear him rustle his straw and paw the ground and grate his horn as he lashed at the door of the pen?

Mike came into the scullery, grim-faced, washed, came in to them, poured himself a cup of coffee, cut a slice of pasty, and began to eat, without saying a word.

'Mike? What's happening?'

Liz wanted to go and look, to see what they were doing to her mare. Was Honey alive, or lying there dead too, her dead foal beside her? What was going on?

'It's a slow job. Dr. Lyndon's not used to operating.

And they had trouble at first with the anaesthetic. And had to talk it all over for a long time. Can't just plunge in ... he had to look at a book, see how the mare's made. ...'

He bit into the food. It seemed a twelvemonth since he'd eaten, not had time for lunch.

'Where are the children?' Joe asked suddenly, startled to find he had completely forgotten them.

'Nora sent a message. She's keeping them tonight. Are you going home, Mike?' Liz asked.

Mike shook his head.

'Be a sitting-up job, all night and tomorrow and mebbe next night too, can't leave the mare alone at all,' Mike said.

'I'll stay,' Lew said. It would be something to do and he didn't want to sleep, to give way to nightmares that he knew would come, to memories of his owd bull, his magnificence and pride. Owd bull, slain in his pride.

The telephone bell made them all jump.

It was the knacker.

'Thought you'd like to know,' the impersonal voice at the other end said, when Joe answered. 'That bull of yours ... must have banged his horn and injured the base of it ... had a dirty great abscess there, almost into his brain. No wonder you had trouble with him. Reckon he'd have had to be put down anyway. ...'

'No wonder he was so cranky,' Mike said, finishing the last of his pasty, gulping down a second cup of coffee, hurrying across the yard, opening the door of the bull-pen to let light flood out, and then fade as the door closed again. None of them could take their eyes off the shut door.

'Reckon I can't go home, neither,' Nat said, and looked wistfully at the table. Liz cut him a big portion from the remains of the pasty, and fetched another mug. Nat withdrew to the window seat. Casey, who had stumbled downstairs, muzzily, seeking company, climbed back into Liz's arms and lay looking up at her with wide eyes, as if wanting her to explain what was happening. The steady stare was quite unnerving. Liz stroked the soft fur, and the cat sighed deeply and turned and settled himself deeper into her lap, still sleepy from the tranquillizer.

It was cold in the kitchen but no one shut the door. Bennie lay across the step, puzzled by the fact that no one seemed to be thinking of going to bed, although the animals had been fed and bedded much earlier than usual. Midge and Tartar were curled together on the rug, Tartar engaged in a deep and detailed and intimate bath that Midge helped along occasionally by a lazy lick with her tongue. His coat cleaned to his satisfaction, Tartar began on hers, and presently his busy tongue inspired Midge to wash too, so that everyone in the room was aware of the soft suck from the two busy little animals.

Joe roused himself.

'Have to shift Honey if we can . . . is her foaling room ready?'

'Done it yestiddy,' said Nat. 'Clean and fresh straw . . . thought she might be early . . . that's a mighty big foal for lil mare. . . .'

It was over two hours before the door of the temporary operating theatre opened. Mike came out, saying something over his shoulder. He walked into the kitchen and glanced at the clock. One o'clock in the morning. What a day. He nodded to Liz.

'All over. Just need to clean them up.'

'Are they O.K.?' Liz was impatient to know.

'Fine foal. As for Honey . . . take a day or two to tell . . . she was pretty exhausted before they started. Good

194

job they did ... we'd have 'ad to pull the foal out bit by bit ... he's enormous, and his foot was curled ... he's a grand little beast. A grey, I reckon.'

A great grey stallion ... Liz thought. What fools people are. If Dave hadn't been there. ...

Mike took water and sponges. At the doorway he looked back.

'Come and see, quickly, and don't bother about the mess ... it looks pretty gruesome ... and then go and get some sleep. I'll sit with her till five, and then you can take over ... and you sleep, too, Lew. Want you with her tomorrow when she's waking and sore and doesn't know what's hit her ... and that time's going to be important.'

They followed him as far as the door of the bull-pen. The mare lay on her side, and Mike had put straw beneath her. She could not be moved for a while. The foal was wet and bloody, but his eyes found the group at the door and stared, blue eyes not focusing yet. His head moved easily, his nostrils sucking greedily at the air that was strange to him, as he looked at the astounding world that had given him so harsh a welcome.

His mother was not awake and ready to instil caution into him, to shelter him from harm. He knew nothing of fear, and sniffed at Ken's hand as he began to sponge away the signs of birth.

'Hope the mare will take to him after that lot,' he said, busy washing the foal. 'It helps the mother to clean it herself ... but we'll face that hurdle when we come to it.'

Liz sighed. A beast that would not take to its own young was always tricky. Sometimes complete rejection followed a difficult birth. With calves or lambs it was often enough to put a dog in with the mother and baby, and Bennie knew just how to chivvy without harming any animal he was asked to treat in this way. The mother instinct, dormant at first usually flared to life when she saw her young under attack, and she would turn on the dog and then take the baby and feed it and clean it.

'Thank you, Dave,' Liz said, catching the doctor's eye. Dave laughed.

'First time I delivered a foal,' he said. 'Never thought to see the day. I've a lot more respect for a vet's job now . . . damned funny shape . . . a horse.'

'I'll finish here,' Mike said. 'Not much left to do and I'd rather be busy than just sitting. Don't fall asleep then.'

Nat had brought in a garden chair and a horse blanket. The mare was clean now, and Nat covered her, avoiding the neatly stitched gash that divided her. She was breathing easily.

They all jumped when Bennie growled as the gate hinge screeched, and a car drove into the yard.

'Who on earth?' asked Joe of no one in particular.

The stranger was tall and fair, with a stubble of strong beard that needed a shave. His blue eyes looked them over, and picked out Ken.

'I'm Jock McKie,' he said, his voice faintly and pleasantly accented. 'Remember? Five years ago, at the Bridlington conference. Your mother got hold of me, and thought I'd better look in and see how things were, and drive you home. She says she's driving you to the hospital first thing in the morning.'

He bent to look at the mare.

'How in hell did you operate with only one arm?'

Ken grinned, his face drawn and exhausted, but showing his elation. All had gone well after all.

'We had a real midwife. Our local doctor,' he said, introducing Dave, and Jock laughed.

'Bet that was a change for you,' he said.

'It was,' Dave answered. 'But do you know, I'm rather proud of that foal.'

He patted the little beast on the head and walked outside. It would be good to get to bed. He was glad he did not have to remain.

'I'll come back at milking time. She ought to be all right till then, but ring me if you want me,' Jock said, and Mike nodded. He knew what to watch for, and luckily the vet's house was only a couple of miles away ... ten minutes in the car at this time of night.

It was hardly worth undressing. Only three and a half hours to milking time. They watched Nat and Lew plod into the night, took a last look at the mare and foal, provided Mike with coffee and a rug, and water for the mare to drink, and climbed up stairs that seemed ten times as steep as usual and dropped on top of the bed. Casey came with them and burrowed between them, needing the comfort of people's bodies against his. Liz let him stay in the crook of her arm. It was years since he had slept all night away from the bull and she half expected him to ask to go outside, but he seemed to know that that was useless and no matter how hard he looked the bull was gone for ever.

Lew went home to dream again and again of his proud beauty, his splendid beast, magnificent in his rage; of the night in the quarry when the bull had been meek and quiet and wanting comfort and the many times that Lew's hands and Lew's soft voice had soothed his rousing temper and stilled his anger.

And the dream went on, as the bull stormed over the cobbles, hurling his bulk at the treacherous gun that blared its death note and the splendour faded and the bull's body shrivelled and shrank and became Casey, crying in torment, unable to understand.

Lew woke, shuddering and sweating, to hear the owls hooting to one another. Waking held no promise. The wild trees keened their echo to his mourning and dark clouds hid the watchful moon.

CHAPTER EIGHTEEN

Liz woke to the shrilling alarm. She switched it off hastily. Jo was still asleep. She took her clothes, intending to dress in the kitchen. Casey wailed, and she grabbed him, closed the door gently behind her and hurried downstairs.

Mike came in to the kitchen as she was pouring water on to the coffee grounds. He yawned.

'Mare's awake,' he said. 'Want to go and see? I'll finish that and make her a warm mash. Lew's with her. Reckon he never slept a wink. Came back about four this morning. Nat's fetching cows in.'

The morning was chill and grey. A haze lay above the meadows, a small low ghost-mist rising gently to knee height. Casey followed Liz like a shadow. At the doorway to the bull-pen he wailed again. She lifted him and went inside.

Honey was lying in the straw, her dark eyes wide open. The foal lay against her, luxuriating in her warmth, his small head stretched up to look at his mother. The mare licked his damp nose. Liz relaxed. No trouble here. Honey was proud of her son, asking approval, and Liz knelt and patted the golden brown coat.

'Clever lil mare,' Lew said from the shadows. He

brought a fistful of pony nuts and she ate them from his hand. 'Her's 'ungry.'

When Jock McKie arrived they were all watching the mare eat her mash, as if it was an event never seen before. He grinned at their absorbed faces. He knew just how they felt. He had been anxious himself as he drove through the misty lanes, lest the ordeal had proved too much for her and she was suffering from any of the ill-effects that could follow such an operation.

He examined her carefully. She did not flinch from his exploring hands. The skin around the wound was healthy, no sign of sepsis. She was hungry and thirsty, and before he left her she was on her feet, nosing at the foal that was ready to feed. Mike supervised the process, preventing the little creature from tugging too hard.

'Animals recover fast when they do recover,' Jock said with satisfaction as he sat to share coffee and bacon and eggs. 'Ken's going straight to the hospital at nine for an X-ray. Had to dope him well last night.'

'What with?' Liz asked, stirring her cup, stroking Casey, who had jumped on to her lap the instant she sat down.

'Whisky,' Jock said. 'A good old Scots remedy. What else?'

Liz laughed.

'Liz!' Mike's voice was urgent coming from the scullery, where he had gone to wash his face. He came to the doorway, drying his face and hair with a towel. Nothing like a douche of cold water to wake a man up, he thought.

Liz glanced up anxiously.

'You know what day it is?'

She shook her head.

'Gone clean out of my mind. It's Gymkhana Day. And

no jumps ready. And they're coming at ten to set up the field and the marquee. And Starlight can't jump and Scotty's out of it. Fine show we'll be putting on.'

'Village'll help.' Nat had come in for his coffee. The cattle were waiting outside the milking parlour. Have a drink and then he'd see to them. He'd been to see the foal and come away grinning. Nothing like new life on a farm. Made a man's day. Nice lil piece of horseflesh that. He smacked his lips.

Liz looked at the clock. Couldn't telephone at five-thirty. She'd have to plan. She finished her breakfast and started to make the lists that she had intended to do the day before. Lew could stay with Honey.

The village knew what had happened at Wayman's Corner. Long before Liz had telephoned them, the men were there. The vicar with bread and rolls and butter, and his wife's promise to come soon; Harry Makeride from the Smithy, prepared to put up the jumps and help with the horses; the two Misses Bennett from Hill Cottage, with pasties for everyone's lunch and all the lists that Liz should have made, and their four hands only too willing to turn to anything. Long before the sun was high enough to throw the shadow of the lime tree across the yard the field had begun to look like carnival-like with flags and bunting and the ice-cream van in the corner.

Liz was considerably startled, looking out of the window a little later, to see Roger Leigh arrive with his mother in the little scarlet car.

She did not want to see either of them.

'The nerve of the woman,' she said in fury to the younger Miss Bennett.

'No need to worry,' Miss Bennett observed, watching with considerable satisfaction as a group of people made way for Mrs. Leigh and her son, without turning a head or saying a word.

Roger ran to the ice-cream van, where a group of children had already collected and the vendor, a local man, was doing a brisk trade. His urgent appeals remained unheard, and he returned to his mother, who walked over to the ice-cream van, her face wrathful.

'My son wants an ice-cream,' she said angrily.

'Then mebbe he could find someone that wants to sell him one,' the vanman said. He looked at Roger and grinned. 'We're choosy in these parts.'

Mrs. Leigh flushed suddenly and angrily, and turned on her heel, as the children began to laugh, and nearby adults turned their heads and looked at her. Everyone knew what had happened to cause the bull to run berserk, and the Leighs had never been popular.

The scarlet car zipped off with a flurry of gravel.

'Good riddance,' Nat Martin said, and spat expressively into the grass, before taking the cattle to the far field while Mike dressed Scotty's shoulder and Starlight's hoof, and then took Benty for exercise. He had been training Starlight for a special display, based on his police training. The wretched thing was billed on the programme. He wanted to try and work something out with Benty, but there was very little time and he would have to concentrate on something very simple. The horse could not possibly learn new tricks in one short hour.

By lunch time the place was seething, with children and ponies everywhere and cars parked on the top meadow and the long meadow. The dogs were restless and excited. Tich, independent as ever, went ratting. Casey, who had followed Liz hopelessly from place to place, became bewildered. He had never seen so many legs and feet in all his life. He took refuge in the stable to which Honey had been moved, but Honey was new-mother-nervous and snorted at him and pawed the ground. He remembered his broken leg, which he had gained in just such another situation, and went outside.

A Land-Rover and horse-box drew up, almost under his nose. Casey had had more than enough. There were too many hazards, too much likelihood of a kick or a trodden paw, and even inside the house were more folk than he had ever seen before. He left the farmyard.

He crossed the field, keeping to the edge, diving into the ditch, anxious only to get away, away from men shouting and children squealing and horses calling to one another in excitement, away from the push and the jostle and thrust and the queue for ice-creams and the sudden thump and thunder of the shaking ground as the first horse began to take the jumps.

He sat for a long time on a small bank in the meadow that bordered the brook, watching a butterfly flirting from flower to flower, watching a bird that flew unwisely close, observing waving grass and the furtive movement of a creeping mouse. The sun was warm and he was comfortable, but the loneliness inside him could not be appeased. He had looked for the bull all morning. He had cried to Liz to find him, but Liz had taken no notice, merely stroking him and petting him as if that was what he wanted. Perhaps the bull was in the field by the water. Casey got up, stretched thoughtfully, and walked on.

Weeks before, so long ago that he had forgotten her, he had met a tabby cat beside the brook. He played with her for three days, mated with her, and then did not see her again. She was Silver Cat, from the smallholding at Gallows End, where her owner, a small fierce man with a bristling moustache, destroyed her litters by banging the kittens' heads against the wall, never bothering to see if she was there watching or not.

Silver Cat had this litter in an old otter holt, under a twisted tree root by the river bank. It was warm and dry and comfortable, but it was unwise. The kittens were lively, active, and curious, every one with Casey's love of life and Casey's undying curiosity. Before long Silver Cat had to move them, away from the water that bubbled and hissed too close to them. She had moved three. They lay together, mischievous small bundles of fur. The fourth had tried to follow her. Now he and Silver Cat were marooned. He had fallen into the stream. Silver Cat had climbed down and rescued him. But, with him in her mouth and the treacherous water behind her, she was unable to jump up the bank. She scrabbled at the earth frantically with her claws, but the mud was slippery, and each time she fell back. She was tiring, and her hind legs were wet and she hated water, but she was not going to give in.

Casey, wandering along beside the brook, peered down and saw her. He was puzzled because she would not jump. He landed light beside her, and nosed her, and in a sudden blinding moment caught the scent of the kitten, his own scent, mixed with Silver Cat's scent. Silver Cat tried to climb again and again she slipped. Casey sat and thought.

He jumped to the top of the bank, and looked down. He flattened himself and stretched his head. Silver Cat stood on her hind legs. He could just reach. With silken soft grip he took his small son and, relieved of her burden, Silver Cat jumped up beside him and purred and rubbed against him and stretched.

Casey followed her to the bracken clump where the other kittens were hidden. This would not do, he felt obscurely, afraid of danger, sure that there must be some other, safer place than this. He began to walk back to the farm, carrying his son. Silver Cat watched him, and then picked up one of the other kits, and followed.

It was a long, hot slow job. They did not leave any kitten alone for long. A few yards' walk, and then the babies were put side by side, and the two cats returned to bring the others to them. The journey took most of the afternoon and half of the evening and the farmyard was quiet when they reached it at last. Everyone, including Nora, Mike's wife, was tucking into the huge meal that Liz had prepared to celebrate the end of the Gymkhana and the success of Mike's fierce gallops, complete with home-made lance with which he speared a ring hanging from a pole, and Jane's rosette, won with Candy. Nobody saw the cats cross the yard. Nobody saw them vanish into the darkness of Scotty's stable.

Mike, going out to bed the horses and have a last look at the invalids, and a last word with the smith who had offered to sit up with Honey that night and make sure all was well, heard Casey call to him as he walked into the stable. He looked around. There was no sign of the cat, but the yowl came again, from a place close to the hay-rack.

There was an old box there, into which had dropped generous portions of Scotty's hay. There, lying close around her kittens, was Silver Cat. She swore at Mike softly, daring him to come close. Casey lay in the straw, one paw holding the biggest kitten firmly, his tongue cleaning off the river mud that soiled the little beast's back.

'Well, I'll be damned,' Mike said, and went back to the kitchen.

'Casey's got a family,' he said.

'Casey's got what?' Joe said, unbelieving.

'He's brought home Silver Cat from the smallholding and four kits, and I'll swear they're his kits. He's baby sitting.'

The children jumped down from the table.

'Gently,' Mike warned. 'Silver Cat's not trustful like our cats.'

Liz grinned at Joe. Mike felt he belonged, and she was glad of it. She followed the others into the yard.

Casey was hungry, but was not going to desert his young. He had always adored kittens, playing endlessly with those from Midge's many litters, and these were his. He could sense that, in each small body. He felt a vast protectiveness, and growled at Jane when she put a hand down to touch.

Liz brought food for both cats. Silver Cat was starving and wolfed hers fast and then turned on Casey, spitting and swearing, driving him from his own plate. He watched her meekly. Liz brought him another helping, but Silver Cat took that too, and at last Casey was persuaded to come outside and eat in peace. He returned at once to his brood.

Late that night Liz watched the clouds that ruffled the sky, saw the soft-flighted owl wing across to the barn, heard the cattle lowing in the field, kissed the sleeping children, lingering for a moment by their beds, and stood in the doorway.

The yard was quiet. Gone was the brooding menace and the fear. The bull would not trouble them again, and yet, in spite of her hatred of him, and her certainty that he would do them harm, she missed his presence. It was not the same without him.

Casey came to her, stepping delicately. He rubbed against her legs, acknowledging her. He went to the bullpen and wailed, an eerie long drawn out yowl that made

Liz shiver. Silver Cat, puzzled, nosed him daintily and mewed, and the two cats stood together rubbing heads before going inside into the dark stable.

Liz went to shut Scotty up for the night. She stroked his nose and fed him his three sugar lumps. She could see Casey's green eyes glowing in the dark. Beneath them were a pair of small slit eyes, half-closed. The tiny cat was curled close against his father, returning only to his mother when he wanted food.

Casey lowered his head and licked the soft black fur possessively. He had said his last farewell to the memory of the bull. He would never forget him, never understand what had happened, but he had found a new source of content. His purr throbbed on the air.

Next morning he went hunting and brought Silver Cat the biggest mouse he could find and watched her devour it. He watched over the kittens, more anxious than their mother to guard them from harm. Baby care made him hungry. He foraged in the pantry and stole an end of ham.

He fought over it with Tartar, and went to find Lew and show him a damaged paw, which Tartar had bitten in a moment of fury, being as big a devotee of ham as Casey.

Lew bathed the paw and dressed it with penicillin, pushing the nozzle of the tube well into the bite. Casey licked it, his expression pathetic.

'Born to trouble,' Lew said.

Liz, hearing him, sighed deeply. Everything was back to normal. She looked out across the tree-lined field at the grazing cattle, and then over the cobbled yard, where Honey was watching Jane and Peter squabble over a ball game, at the far field, where Nat was driving the tractor, and at the near meadow, where Joe was mending a fence.

A bird sang from the coppice and Casey chattered at him, and then picked up his smallest son and returned him purposefully to the dark sanctuary of the stable. Casey had had a lot of trouble in his own short life. But he could keep his younglings safe.

He put the kitten down in the straw and sauntered towards Liz, aware of a job well done. Behind him, a small and enthusiastic fluff of black fur staggered out of the stable, and yowled. Casey turned and smacked the kitten with an angry paw and picked it up again.

Liz laughed.

'Casey's going to be very busy,' she said, and went indoors to make tea and to ponder on the strangeness of the past year, and the way in which horror had come and passed again, and left her with nothing but good fortune.

Joe came in from the field.

'Have you ever thought,' he asked, 'what life here is going to be like with Tartar and five Caseys?'